Love

at

Turtle Dove Inn

The Inheritance Bay • Book One

SUSAN WARNER

Love
at
Turtle Dove Inn

One

"It's not happening, young lady, so keep walking."

Riley Jackson stood in the doorway of the motel's main office, with Merlin by her side. Anger and disbelief with how things were going coursed through her body as the older gentleman sitting behind the counter looked down his nose at her. She could feel his disdain like the slight chill that filled the February air from Inheritance Bay, if the brochure was to be believed.

Next to her, Merlin, her thirteen-year-old black Rottweiler, looked up at her with his sad eyes as if he understood the words coming from the motel owner.

"I'm not asking for a handout. I can pay extra for his stay," Riley said, holding on to Merlin's leash. Sometimes when he was spooked or unhappy, he could backpedal, and if she weren't prepared, they'd both be going backward.

"You don't have enough money, little lady. Look at that monster. He'd tear up my room. Business isn't so good anyway, and it'd have to come out of pocket, no way.

5

Just turn around. You're pretty, but my pockets can't afford it."

What was wrong with men?! She had just left a boss who didn't understand that just because she worked in his restaurant didn't mean he could order her to have a relationship with him. When she had received a letter offering a new chance here in Inheritance Bay, she figured she was finally going to get a break. Riley had read the letter twice to make sure it was real and called the number. Once her identity had been confirmed, she was told she could stay at the Sunny Motel, and she would be picked up from there.

All of it had been arranged by a woman named Marjorie. According to her, the town was offering prior residents and their family an opportunity to come back if they would pick a business do an internship and then the town would help them to open a business and get resettled.

The letter was perfectly timed. Riley was tired of her current job. The advances from her boss were bordering on harassment, and Riley knew her days there were numbered. Her boss was a pain, the pay was low, and there was no chance she'd ever do anything else in the little restaurant except cook, and on some rare occasions, be allowed to pick up a shift at the bed and breakfast next to the restaurant. Riley wanted more, and when she told the woman on the phone about her restaurant and hotel experience, Marjorie said they had a perfect opportunity. So with no better prospects, she packed up herself and Merlin, the only male she trusted, into her gray Land Rover and set out for Inheritance Bay, Long Island.

It was going to be a change, but Riley was ready for one. She'd have the opportunity to learn the business in a small town with its own bay. They said they'd provide room and board for her. The most important thing in all of this was that she and Merlin would be together.

Now that she had arrived, it seemed as though her bad luck was catching up with her.

"I was invited here. I got a letter from Marjorie Talton. She said I could come and that we could get lodging here."

The gruff man gave Merlin another look and then shivered.

"Well, Marjorie didn't say nothing about pets. I don't do pets, and they don't like me," he said as he folded his arms across his spindly chest.

Riley clenched her teeth and got a hold of her temper. She could hear the man closing his mind to being rational. If he was like this all of the time it was no wonder that pets didn't like him. He didn't seem to be a very likable fellow at the moment. The motel owner—she supposed he was a manager or the owner—sounded nothing like the nice woman who had emanated nothing but kindness about her situation and gratefulness that she was willing to come.

She had been on the road for the last six hours. Merlin could travel, but he would need a break and some time to stretch his legs. Realizing the motel owner wasn't going to be helpful, she backed out and started back to her truck.

Riley started to second guess herself. There was a ball of dread building in the pit of her stomach. What was she going to do? This wasn't her home town or even her home state of Florida. She had done the one thing her father had warned her not to do. Riley had put all her eggs in one basket and come to Inheritance Bay. She had given away or sold any possessions that couldn't fit into her truck. Riley had decided not to waste money on storage in a place she had no intention of ever seeing again. With the majority of her money sewn into different parts of her jacket, suitcases in the truck, and nowhere to stay, what was she going to do?

Merlin whined, and Riley looked down at her bestie and smiled. She walked him to a nearby patch of grass so he could relieve himself. While she watched him walk around, do his business, and then rest in a patch of sun, she knew she'd find a way.

"Well, Merlin, it looks like we are going to have to make a change again," she said. Merlin glanced over at her and then laid his head on his crossed paws.

"I know this isn't what I planned, but we will make this work. Don't we always?" Riley waited for Merlin to pick up his head. She looked around and had to admit the motel owner was right about one thing. There wasn't a lot of business around here. Riley remembered seeing some stores a couple of blocks away. She'd leave her truck and take Merlin on a walk. She was pretty sure her truck was safe, and she needed the time to think.

She threw a couple of blue pooper-scooper bags in her pocket for Merlin and started down the street. The crisp air helped her to clear her mind. Save for the lack of people on the street of Inheritance Bay, it looked like something straight out of a Norman Rockwell painting. As she walked down the block, she assumed she was getting closer to the water because the errant breeze was coming in regular intervals. If she stayed, she was going to have to get a heavier jacket. Riley cleared her mind. The question wasn't *if* she stayed but *how* she was going to make this work.

She looked at Merlin, who was keeping pace with her, and smiled. Some days were good for Merlin, and others not so much. He was a rescue that a friend of hers had been fostering. When the former friend told her that she would have to take Merlin back to the pound, where he would probably be put down because he was an older dog, Riley wound up adopting him.

As Riley went past first an ice cream parlor and then what looked like a convenience store, her spirits picked up. She could get some food for her and Merlin. Riley had learned long ago to take care of things one at a time. Food first and then shelter, she hoped.

Riley found a light post and tied Merlin to the post. He looked at the post and then at her.

"I'm going in to get food, so don't give me that look." Merlin shook and then tucked his tail and sat down next to the post. Riley was about to lecture Merlin on guilt when she heard her name.

"Riley? Is that you, Riley?" Marjorie Talton asked her. Riley turned and pasted on her best smile. Marjorie was the contact Riley had reached out to on the letter. They had done a couple of zoom calls so she knew what Marjorie looked like but wasn't the same as seeing her in person.

Marjorie was the epitome of a woman who aged well. Her figure was willowy, time had been kind to her, and her smile was ever-present. The only hint that Marjorie might be around her late fifties was her neck. The neck never lied.

"Hello, Marjorie."

"Oh, my goodness, you're here. Has the time slipped me by? I thought you weren't supposed to be here for another day or two."

"I thought coming a bit early to get settled would be prudent."

"Ahh, I see. Have you been to the motel yet?"

"Yes," Riley said hesitantly.

Riley could see the distress on Marjorie's face.

"I have to admit. I hadn't told Larry about your dog. I thought I'd pay him first and then tell him. I take it he was not pleased."

Riley knew she was nibbling on her lower lip, but she couldn't stop the nervous habit.

"He wasn't pleased. In fact, he said—"

"Don't even bother to repeat what the old coot said. I'm so sorry if he was rude. I'll go speak to him. Let me see if I can reason with him. If not, this may be a challenge. Larry is the only open motel in the Bay. I'll try to get him to reconsider, but if not, we may have to re-evaluate the pet situation."

There it was, a one-two punch that took Riley's breath away. Re-evaluate the pet situation? She wasn't sure what Marjorie meant, but the panic that flared in Riley's body and the adrenaline rush that pushed her brain to think twice as fast wasn't going to re-evaluate a thing when it came to Merlin.

"Why don't you speak with Larry first, and we'll go from there," Riley suggested.

"You're absolutely right. No sense in borrowing trouble if we don't have to." Marjorie smiled and then made her way back down the four blocks Riley had just walked. Riley could feel the heat behind her eyes. If another thing happened, she'd just fall down and cry. She wanted to hide, but she had to get Merlin's food. She wasn't even concerned for herself. Riley wasn't sure she could eat a thing anyway. She looked down at Merlin and nodded.

"We've got this, old man. You stay and let me go get you some grub." Riley looked at the few cars on the road and the four-way stop that seemed like it was the middle of town. There was a sports BMW on the road. It looked out of place in the little town. She patted Merlin on the head and then walked to the store front.

She had taken four steps when she saw the light turn green, and then a truck crossed the intersection with the sports car behind it. She saw the truck go over what looked like a small crater in the road, and then as the sports car tried to pass the truck, it hit the same ditch and sounded its horn. The sound jolted Riley, and then she turned to see Merlin had jumped up as well. Merlin was backing up trying to get off of the light post an inadvertently putting his rear end into the street. The sports car was swerving, trying to go around the ditch. Then Riley saw that the sports car was heading straight for Merlin's hindquarters, which were stepping off the curb and into the street.

This couldn't be!

"Merlin!" she yelled, frantic to grab her bestie. She had just leapt for Merlin and had her arms about his neck

11

when she felt him go off-center and fall towards her. She thought the sports car had slowed down enough, but it hadn't been a complete stop. Riley felt a weight hit her shoulder but she was sure it was Merlin. The only thing Riley could think about was protecting her old friend as much as possible.

Conner Sanders's hands tightened on the steering wheel as he mentally beat himself up. If he hadn't been in his sports car, there would have been no way he could have stopped that quickly. Still, it wasn't quick enough. The dog had come out of nowhere, or at least his butt had. Then he saw the woman going for the dog.

Of all the things that could happen to him in this town. He couldn't believe that his attempt to avoid a ditch had put him here. If only he had known, he would have let his car drive right through the ditch to spare the dog and the woman.

He had seen the large truck in front of him bobble up and down letting him know there was something in the wrong in front of him. Conner's thought was to avoid the ditch. Then when he had swerved the car just enough to avoid the ditch he saw the dog and woman. The worse moment was when he felt the tap on his car.

He heard moaning as he exited the car. Moaning had to be better than silence. Conner strode to the front of his car. He needed to be as calm as possible. Conner knew, even when he was panicked, to present confidence. It was one of the many things he knew and practiced being the owner of a multi-million dollar software finance company. The source of the moans was coming from the woman. He wondered why no one was attending to her. When he took a step towards her, he heard the low growl. Conner held his hands out in front of him. It was clear the dog was hers, and he wasn't feeling very friendly. Even tied to the pole there wasn't a clear way to get to the woman with the dog standing guard.

"There, there boy. I just want to get a look at her," Conner said in a calm voice. For a moment, it looked like the hulking beast was going to step aside, but then a couple of other people came walking up, and any minuscule headway he had made was gone. Back in the place of the reasonable giant was the devoted watchdog.

He pulled out his phone and dialed one for the saved number of the sheriff. It was one of the pluses when you bought a third of a town. Conner couldn't tell you what the sheriff looked like but he could get him on the phone. Conner didn't wait for the pleasantries. This line was for him and if he used it both parties knew it wasn't a social call.

"I need someone to come down here and pick up a dog. I've hit a young woman, and it seems her dog is on the defense."

"Done."

He could see the woman's chest moving up and down, and that, coupled with an occasional moan, gave him hope. Every time the woman moaned, the dog bent down and gave her face a lick. Conner could see he was a gentle giant, or at least he was with her.

He was anxious to get to the woman, but the dog wouldn't budge. It was only moments, but it felt like hours before the cops came with the rope leashes for the dog. One of them pulled out a carrier case, but when they saw the behemoth, they shook their heads and put the case back in the trunk.

Since the dog wouldn't move from her side it was easy for the police to loop the dog with multiple leashes. When the leash tightened, the dog sat and wouldn't budge. Looping the dog was one thing, but actually getting him to move, that was looking like a whole new beast. One of the officers reached around to untie the dog from the post. When that was done, they tried to pull the dog along. When the dog started to resist, Conner told both cops to stop.

He saw the dog constantly looking from the cops to the fallen woman.

"Okay big guy. I'm going to take a big chance here, and hopefully, I won't get my face taken off for it," Conner murmured.

"Mr. Sanders, let us do our job," the officer said warily.

Conner moved slowly around the beast and ignored the officers. Conner had built a financial empire based on his instincts, and right now, they were saying for him to take a chance. He was moving slowly, and he was more aware in this moment than ever before. It wasn't surprising to him how aware he felt. It was the same life charged moment he got before he made an important deal. It was funny to have the feeling and no money was involved.

"Good boy," he murmured as he reached out to the woman dressed in blue jeans and a black sweater.

"Come on, little lady, get up so your protector doesn't decide I'm not doing what he wants me to do," he said as he knelt next to her on the sidewalk.

Behind him, he could hear the officers trying to make sense of what had happened.

"I know we've been working on the roads, but I told them to start with the main road. I can't believe it happened to him of all people," the first officer commented to another.

"It's the luck this town has had—just bad," the other officer murmured.

Conner didn't have time to address the officers. He was aware of the sentiment in the town. The common sentiment was he was a plague that was making a bad situation worse. In truth, he didn't understand the issue they all seemed to have anyway. Conner couldn't focus on their problems right now. Right now his attention was completely focused on the young lady before him. There were a lot of things that Conner didn't do well, however the one thing he did exceptionally well was focus. At this moment all of his focus was on making sure the woman was okay. He had made his success on being able to focus, and that was what he was going to do now.

"Mr. Sanders, please pull back," the officer said a little firmer, hoping to move Conner away from the situation. He heard the faint whimpering of a woman in the crowd.

"Oh my, oh my, is that Riley? Poor girl!" an older voice said.

Conner had no time for the foolishness of the officers or the pity of the town. Having money hadn't deprived him of his faculties to act in emergency situations. What? Did they think that he couldn't assist in an emergency with a real person because his eyes looked at financials and built the wealth of some of the leading people in show business and politics? He ignored them all when the woman on the ground started to open her eyes.

The woman reached out, and her hand ran into Conner's face.

"Merlin?" she moaned.

Then her lashes opened, and she blinked twice as if she weren't sure what she was looking at. Her eyes were a rich brown that looked like melted chocolate. They had the glow of silk and a pull that he couldn't seem to resist. He was only distracted from her eyes by the feel of her hand on his cheek. He knew she hadn't meant to touch him, but her hands were just as smooth as the silk he was imagining. Then she pulled back, and the words she was saying suddenly became louder and clearer.

Looking from side to side, she twisted.

"Merlin? Merlin?"

The beast nudged Conner in the back, and he lost his balance and fell to the side. When the dog went towards the woman, the officers tightened their grip, but Conner waved them off. It was too late anyway. He supposed this was Merlin, and if he wanted to do some damage, he had plenty of time to do so.

The woman threw her arms around Merlin and then began to run her hands over him. Conner could see the dog meant more to her than her own status. She still hadn't gotten up from the ground.

"You're Riley?"

As if realizing that there were other people around her, she looked at Conner and then tried to sit up.

16

"Hold on there. I want you to sit up but not too fast. I think—"

"You think? Who thought to put these rough leashes on Merlin?" she said indignantly. "I don't need your help unless it's removing these things off of my baby."

"Listen, Riley. You need a doctor to look at you because I think I hit you when you dove in to protect your dog," he said.

"He hit her?" the question reverberated through the crowd.

"Figures he would," someone else commented. Conner didn't have time for town foolishness.

"How do you feel?" he asked.

"Like a very expensive car hit me," Riley quipped. "Listen, I'm good. I'm a little banged up, but I'm good."

She tried to sit up, and Conner could see her wince as she did so. He had already speed-dialed the doctor, so he knew she'd be here soon.

"I'm glad you think you're okay, but it would be negligent and illegal of me to let you go."

Riley gave him a long look and then seemed to look behind him. When he turned, the doctor was there in her white coat. The doctor had a black bag with her and didn't look too happy to be here. She looked young, like she was fresh out of college but hardly med school.

When he would have questioned her, she just turned her attention to her patient. She didn't even ask Conner to move. She just nudged him and started to ask Riley questions and take her vitals.

"I'd like her to go to the hospital," the doctor said over her shoulder.

It was like the dog understood. Merlin lay down next to Riley and whined. Conner wasn't a dog person. As a child, he had suffered from allergies that had made having a pet problematic at best. Certainly, being an orphan didn't encourage any of his other foster families to get him a pet. By the time the Sanders adopted him, Conner had all but given up on the idea of finding a family that would keep him. He bent down and placed his hand atop Merlin's head. Merlin lifted his head, gave him a look, and then focused on his mistress.

"Do be careful, Mr. Sanders," the matronly Marjorie said from behind him. He stood up and gave her a reassuring smile.

"He seems pretty calm as long as Riley is up. You know her?" he murmured, not wanting his voice to carry over the doctor who was still asking Riley questions.

"Oh yes, she's part of the program to relocate past members. She came early, we originally thought to pair her with Larry, but he doesn't like dogs. I'll find something for her to do, though."

Conner looked at Riley and thought about how she had gotten off to a rotten start in Inheritance Bay.

The doctor finally stood up.

"I'll say it again. I think she should go to the hospital. I can do some things here, but I'd like to watch her overnight."

"You're the doctor," Conner asked skeptically.

Folding her hands over her chest she cocked her head to the side.

"My name is Doctor Carrie Egbert. I'm the doctor, the pharmacist, and in a pinch, the science teacher. Welcome to Inheritance Bay, Mr. Sanders."

18

Was she hoping to hit him up for money? Her timing could be worse.

"The road is a problem. My brother is on the renovations board so we can reach out to him about when this part is scheduled. It's hard to get work done with so few and so little. I know the town mayor; I'm sure she'll cover the hospital cost for the young lady."

He heard the words and thought they sounded forced. Did she think he was going to wield his name to make things happen or disappear? While they were talking, the ambulance showed up.

"It appears she is going to the hospital," Conner said with a raised brow.

Carrie smiled. "I love a man with commonsense."

The EMTs got out of the truck to pick up Riley.

"Stop, I can't leave Merlin!"

The EMTs looked at Carrie. Carrie shook her head. "Nope, not gonna happen. Pets are against hospital policy."

Riley tugged Conner towards her. When he bent down, Riley took off her jacket.

"Listen, this is all your fault. Take my jacket and keep it next to Merlin. He'll be good for a couple of days if need be."

"Wait—" Conner began.

"There's no time to wait. He let you touch him, so you're it. You take care of my baby, or I'll hunt you down. Do you hear me?"

"How can I refuse such a request?"

Riley turned to Merlin. "Merlin, stay with him. Momma will be back soon," she said after she gave Merlin a big hug.

19

Riley nodded, and the EMTs took her away. In minutes the street was clear, and Conner was holding on to Riley's jacket, and Merlin was looking in the direction the ambulance had gone.

Conner couldn't help but think about the large beast next to him and how he was probably allergic to him. He sighed. He'd never had any luck with women. He could predict numbers but women, he just shook his head at a loss.

Conner untied Merlin and then called his name.

"Okay, Merlin. I am going to see your owner in the hospital. I'm going to call my assistant to meet us there, and you will like her," Conner said to Merlin. Merlin gave him a sideways look and then turned back to gaze down the road.

Conner dangled the jacket in front of Merlin. The dogged perked up right away and looked at Conner.

"Okay, old man, let's go," Conner said. He walked Merlin to his car and opened the back door. Merlin jumped into the car, and Conner nodded. This wasn't going to be as bad as he thought. He went to the driver's side, and just as he was taking his seat, Merlin climbed into the passenger side seat.

"You have got to be kidding. Get in the back," Conner said. He took Riley's jacket and tossed it into the back of the car. Merlin looked at the jacket and then back at him. Conner closed the door and leaned his head against the headrest.

Here he was, stuck in his car with a behemoth of a dog who was looking at him as if he had the problem. Conner called his assistant, who was in town, and asked her to meet him at the hospital. When she commented that she had to make a stop by the inn and he would be waiting, he assured her that wouldn't be the case. In fact, he didn't think he would make it anywhere in a timely fashion with Merlin in the car. He had precious cargo in his car, and he would be going very slowly. When he hung up the phone, Merlin gave him a look and then looked over his shoulder, almost as if to point him in the right direction.

Conner didn't like surprises. He planned everything. He hadn't planned on doing anything but going to Turtle Dove Inn and making sure all the arrangements were good for his parents. However, it was his fault, and Riley had entrusted her beloved animal to him. Trust was important to Conner. Before the Sanders, a lot of people had abused his trust. The Sanders had taught him to value trust when it was given, especially when it was given with no guarantees or proof it would be honored.

He started his BMW convertible that boasted going from zero to sixty in less than five seconds and drove it fifteen miles an hour on the side streets to make sure nothing jolted the precious cargo he had been trusted with. His thanks was Merlin leaning his wet nose on the window as the car moved.

Two

"I'm your mother, and you have to tell me," Portia Sanders said on the phone. Conner was about three blocks from the hospital. When the phone rang, Merlin had lifted his head but didn't seem spooked. Conner had answered it, and his mother's voice had surrounded him in the cabin of his car.

Conner was happy that she had called. He found that he needed to ground himself after the incident with Riley.

"Hello, Mom."

Portia Sanders was a retired project manager. She always told him being a project manager was her training before she started adopting kids. When it became clear that Portia couldn't have children, she and Steven Sanders had decided to share their love with six foster children that they would up adopting. His mother was the epitome of love. She welcomed everyone and thing.

He was glad that this call was hands-free and no video; otherwise, she'd start giving him all sorts of to dos to make Merlin comfy.

"I know our anniversary is coming up, and you've planned something. You know you don't need to. We have all that we need with you. But since you've gone this route, it's time to confess to your mother."

Conner smiled to himself when he thought about all the times she had sidled up with him so they could share secrets. He had shared his secret about being able to count any number, and she hadn't made fun of him. He had been seven.

"You know I'd do anything for you, Mom. I want this to be special, so I can't confess this time."

Portia laughed. "I had to try. Seriously, Conner, I know how busy your schedule is. It's the first quarter, and business is at a pivotal point. We can celebrate our anniversary at the house."

It was just another reason he adored his mom. She understood his business and never made him feel bad for wanting to work. One of the reasons his company was so successful was because it was playing to him, not work. At least, that was what it usually felt like. He'd had a change of heart last December.

He hadn't told anyone—especially not his mother.

"How's Dad?" he asked, hoping to keep her distracted. His mom had a talent of knowing when something was wrong or being hidden from her. He hadn't spent as much time with her this past year as he had been dealing with his own personal problems that he didn't want to burden anyone with.

"Your father is just fine. You know, sometimes I think if it were possible, he would have married a golf ball if he could have." He could hear the smile in her voice, and it only amplified the sense of loss and failure he felt from this past year. "I thought I would have empty-nest syndrome when all of you left home, but then your father was kind enough to remind me that I was minding the nest for him before you all arrived.

His parents were the example of what Conner aspired to. They were honest, respected one another, and loved unconditionally. He wasn't so idealistic to think they never had issues or problems, but whatever they were, he knew they would work them out together.

Conner had wanted that with Tammy.

"So, about the surprise?" his mother prodded.

"I can tell you that you will need to get on a plane."

"On a plane? Conner, do we need passports? I don't know where your dad's is and—"

"No, Mom. To get there, you need to fly from Florida but not leave the country."

"Ooo, well, how long will it—?"

"I know you, Mom. If I give you too many clues, you will figure it all out. I want it to be a surprise."

"If you're sure this isn't going to be too much of an issue?" she asked.

"Not at all. I am giving you a surprise, but it always does more for me to see you both and the rest of the gang at some time besides Christmas and Thanksgiving."

"Okay then. I'll let it be. I'll see you soon. I can't wait until we are together."

When Conner hung up the phone, he looked to the side to see Merlin looking at him. He wanted to commiserate with the dog that maybe this idea had been overarching and ambitious. He had to admit he thought he was going to be doing this with a partner, but the idea still held even after Tammy left. He had come up with the idea from a photo he had seen of his parents when they had both just graduated college.

His parents had once lived here but hadn't been back. All the people they knew had moved on, or they had lost contact. When Conner saw a picture of his parents here, they had nothing and still had the same look in their eyes today. The only reason he had bought so much property in Inheritance Bay was to buy the Turtle Dove Inn. It had been the place his parents had their honeymoon. His mom always talked about it and how they were so fortunate to find happiness.

When he found the old picture, he had been with Tammy still, and he thought the inn would be a romantic place for them too. Instead, he found out that the magic wasn't transferable, and Tammy wanted nothing to do with the place. So Conner had let it run on its own, and it had some business but nothing that would make it profitable.

Now that the time was getting closer, he was wondering if this was just an example of a bad decision that people made when they let their emotions run amok. Maybe all of his siblings couldn't be under the same roof for a week. Maybe Tammy was right about this too, that proximity bred contempt.

He was glad that he had gotten his mom off the phone. He knew that the next conversation would have been about him paying to get everyone here. So far, he had managed to avoid the conversation by saying it was a part of the surprise, but Portia wouldn't be put off forever.

Another car pulled up as he arrived, and out came his assistant's husband, James Pekson. A smile came to Conner's mouth when he saw James. James was old enough to be his father. Conner had hired James as part of the Veteran employment program. It had been one of the smartest moves he had made early in his career.

"Conner?" James said as he approached the BMW. James was busy looking in the passenger's seat. "Is that what I think it is?"

Conner cracked Merlin's window and then exited the car. He walked over to James and gave him the keys.

"His name is Merlin, and I ran into his owner."

"Was the car damaged?" James asked.

Conner shook his head. "No, I hit a person, lightly, but enough. She's here. That's her dog, and I need to check on her. I need you to stay while I go."

"Of course, I'll watch him."

Conner patted James on the back and then turned to go into the hospital. Conner was so grateful he had people like James in his life. James was more like his second family now than an employee. Not that he lacked family. As the last adopted child for the Sanders, he had one brother and five sisters.

Conner had built Wealth Builders, Inc. on his instincts and long hours. To do that, his family had needed to understand the holidays where he sent gifts but couldn't show. The only time he spent any time with women was when he visited with his mom or sisters. Through it all, his family had been supportive. All of his siblings had sent cards and flowers for his accomplishments.

He thought he was going to be able to show them that

he had seen their example and was going to follow it by having a family now that he had gotten to a certain point, but that wasn't to be.

His plan didn't include all of the gifts he wanted to give to his parents for their anniversary, but at least they'd all be together. That was, of course, if he could make sure that Riley and Merlin were taken care of as well.

It was amazing to Riley how hospitals and jails seemed so much alike. You couldn't really get up and leave once you were admitted to either one of them. They both claimed they were doing what was best for you and everyone else, and all of them seemed to have a warden. The warden could be a prison guard or a floor nurse, but both of them were vigilant in keeping you in your room.

It wasn't like she didn't appreciate what the professionals did, but she had no good memories attached to hospitals or prisons. Her father had died in a hospital. She was never sure what had happened to change her dad, besides the death of her mother when she was younger. She didn't know the man he was in Inheritance Bay, but the father who had raised her was in and out of jail. She spent more time with women her dad was with than with him.

"I feel fine," Riley said to every doctor who had come in with a magic clipboard. They all asked the same questions.

"Any pain or stiffness in movement?"

"No, none. I just want to get to my dog," Riley said.

All of the doctors nodded and then left. For a moment, Riley wondered if they were seeing if she would change her story. Finally, the doctor that brought her came into her room.

"Thank goodness you came. You'll be able to help me," Riley said with relief in her voice. She could see the slight smile on the doctor's face, and something in Riley said that this look did not bode well for her.

"You're right. I can help you, and I am doing so now."

Riley shook her head. "No, me staying here is just a huge waste of time, and to be honest, I'm not even sure I can afford this."

The doctor nodded and then took a seat on the bed next to Riley.

"Well, I'm a doctor, so this looking at you thing? It's what I wake up in the morning for. As for the expense, that is all being taken care of by Mr. Sanders."

Riley could tell by the smile that spread across the doctor's face that she thought the news she had just delivered would be welcomed. However, in Riley's head, she needed to get out of the hospital as soon as possible. Who wanted to owe a creep who would call animal control on her Merlin?

"I'm going to be in town for a bit. I was on my way to find a place," Riley said.

The doctor laughed. "Did you show up to Larry's with your dog? He's allergic, so he's not going to give you a place to stay, and I have to tell you that pickings are slim in Inheritance Bay. There is the Sanders' place, but like everything else in this town, he closed up a viable business for some odd reason."

"Listen, I'm not sure about what Mr. Sanders does or doesn't do, but I'll find something."

The doctor gave her a once over and then shook her head. "If we were in a large town or next to a city, it would be different, but I have to say that I'm not comfortable letting you go without having a night watch on you. In fact, depending on how the watch goes, you may have to stay a couple of days and—"

"Hold on there, let's not jump the gun here," a male voice said from the doorway.

It was him. The doctor stood up from the bed, and Riley looked around her to see if Mr. Sanders was followed by the pitter-patter of four feet. He had that sleek look to him, like all of his clothes were soft and expensive. He didn't look like he worked out, but he still had nice shoulders. Now that she had a name, she would know who to sue.

"Where is Merlin?" she asked, trying not to jump to conclusions about her precious friend.

"He's in the car," Sanders replied.

"Tell me that was your poor attempt at a joke," Riley said, throwing her legs over the side of the bed.

Holding both hands in front of him, he took a step back. "He's in the car. The window is rolled down, and my assistant is watching him while he is in the car."

The doctor stepped aside and gave a small chuckle. "Well, Sanders, you are consistent, throwing money at a situation."

Sanders gave the doctor a confused look and then turned back to Riley.

"I have an idea. As you heard, I have an inn that is under renovation for a special gathering."

The doctor sighed. "Wow, that's what it takes for you to shut down half a town. You want to have a party?" she muttered.

Sanders shook his head.

"It's not just a party. My parents are having their fiftieth anniversary, and they are going spend it here with my siblings."

"You are throwing your parents an anniversary party at the Turtle Dove Inn on one of the busiest weekends for the place? Valentine's Day?"

He nodded. "That's their anniversary." Sanders turned back to Riley. "You and Merlin can stay there. It's empty until my parents arrive. The only people there are my assistants."

Riley was trying to think of a way to answer without sounding rude. "I think I should try to find something else," she said.

"There is nothing else. I know we got off to a bad start—"

"You hit me with your car and then tried to take my dog off to animal control. Yes, I'd say you started out the wrong way."

"I am admitting that I'm responsible, and I want to make amends," he said.

"You should take him up on it. It's one of the few things I've seen him take responsibility for at all in this town," the doctor said snarkily.

Riley was at a crossroads, but she wasn't going to give up without a fight, and at the end of the day, she had to make sure she was doing the best thing for her and Merlin.

"Merlin is an indoor dog," she said like a challenge.

"Of course he is," he answered. "The inn is large enough. Is he housebroken?"

"Yes, he is. He's just old, so he doesn't move as fast as he once did."

"That's not a problem for me," Sanders said.

Riley looked at the doctor, who gave her a nod and then looked back at Sanders.

"Well, then you've got yourself two guests for the night."

The doctor smiled. "I'm glad that is decided. Let me get your paperwork, and you can go," the doctor said, and then she took her leave of the room.

Sanders stood by the door looking over his shoulder and then at her. Riley looked at Mr. Tall-Lean-and-Handsome and thought it would figure she met a man who she thought was attractive, but he'd already tried to kill her. Talk about a pre-requisite for liking a person.

Three

Okay, she had to admit that was the fastest she had ever been released from a hospital. Riley didn't like the idea that she was depending on him. She could see how this man ever so gently seemed to get his way no matter the situation. In less than an hour, she was walking out into the visitors' waiting area.

"No wheelchair?" he asked.

"I had to draw the line somewhere, and it seemed as though the women thought they were doing me a favor by giving me an excuse to lean on you. You may not be very popular, but you've still got your looks," she quipped. Conner cleared his throat, and if she wasn't mistaken, it almost looked as if the man blushed.

"Well, let's be on our way. Maybe it's not too late to save the car," he murmured.

He placed his hand at the small of her back, and she flinched from the touch.

"Did I hurt you?" he asked.

Riley shook her head and kept on moving. How did

you tell a man that it had been so long since she had been escorted by a man that the touch felt foreign? When they walked out the door, she saw Merlin hanging his head out the window. His tongue was lolling to the side, and he didn't look stressed or concerned at all.

An older gentleman came around the car. He wore a smile on his face and seemed like he was a very rough man. All of Riley's thoughts were pushed away when she shook his hand, and in a gentle voice, he said hello and praised what a good job she had done with Merlin. With the pleasantries done, he nodded to Conner and then left them to get into the car. When Riley got into the car, Merlin went to lay down in the back seat. After a few moments of driving, Conner broke the silence.

"Merlin wouldn't get into the back of the car the whole time," he said.

A smile came to Riley's face as she thought it over. "Are you trying to tell me you let Merlin punk you to sit in the front seat?" she asked.

His hands tightened on the wheel. "It wasn't like that. I just tried to help him through a stressful moment by not adding more stress."

She nodded and said, "Mhmm."

"Anyway, I want you to know I settled the bill at the hospital, and there is no one except my two assistants at the inn, so you can pick any room you want to stay in on the first floor."

"I want to thank you, but you don't have to, you know. I'm not going to sue you."

"I appreciate the not suing me, but I'm just concerned about your welfare. I think I can handle the money issues."

Looking at his car and the way several people had said he had bought up the town, she was sure he could afford the money issues as well. When she was sure he would drive the rest of the way in silence, he surprised her by asking her more questions about herself.

"So, where did you come from? I know Marjorie said you came as a result of the relocation letters. You seem a bit young."

Riley laughed. "I seem young? Wow, what are you fifty with a facelift to look like you're in your thirties?"

"Okay, maybe I deserved that one. I'm thirty-two."

"Not that it's polite for a man to ask, but I'm twenty-eight. My dad was the one the letter went to, but he passed away. Marjorie said I could take his place. I worked in a kitchen and can do some hotel work, mostly on the management side."

"I'm sorry about your dad," he said.

"Thank you, but I have to confess we weren't always on the best terms before he passed."

"So it's right before Valentine's Day. What did your romantic interest have to say?"

"Is that your no subtle way of asking me if I'm involved?"

"While you were in the hospital, I had your car towed to the inn, and Larry said you showed up alone, but you never know."

Riley turned towards him and let the indignation flow over her.

"You didn't even know if I would say yes. A bit high-handed of you, don't you think?"

"High-handed? No. My place is the only logical place.

Besides, entertain the idea that the smaller the town, the more we want to help one another out."

Riley didn't say anything. The reason he had mentioned was the very reason she moved here. She wanted a new start for her and Merlin. She was tired of the hostile competitiveness. She was tired of the jobs that went nowhere and the life that seemed to be an existence.

Inheritance Bay was on the tip of Long Island. It was still close enough that she could go into a nearby city as if it were an excursion.

"Was your father your only family?" he asked.

"He was the only one who ever claimed to be related to me. I've got some friends, though. So I guess if this doesn't pan out, I can always go to one of their houses and regroup."

Regroup would be the word, and she'd have to do it quickly. A friend or two wouldn't mind her, but Merlin would be a whole different matter. Just when she was about to tell him not to worry, they passed a sign that said Turtle Dove Inn to the right.

It was a spiral driveway, and it could have been cute had the hedges been done. When they pulled up to the inn, it looked like it was straight from a fairy tale. It was a large cottage with double doors at the front. It was about three stories, and at the very top, there were two stone turtle doves.

In front of the inn, there were two space heaters strategically placed so that the couple who were waiting there for them didn't get cold. In fact, Riley thought that anyone who had to wait there for a taxi wouldn't get a chill at all.

When the car stopped in front of the couple, Conner spoke. "Welcome to Turtle Dove Inn," he said as he stopped the car. When the car came to a complete stop, the couple separated and went to open the driver and the passenger side door.

The woman was a hefty woman with short, curly hair and a face with deep laugh lines. "Hello, I hear you're the one our Conner hit. I have been telling him he should bring a girl home one day, but I didn't think he'd go this far. Welcome to the Turtle Dove."

Riley turned to check on Merlin only to find he was making his way out of the car behind her. Riley was going to have to get his leash. She didn't want Merlin to scare anyone.

"Oh, my goodness, look at this, James! She's got herself an old man."

Riley looked over at the gentleman helping Conner only to discover it was the assistant she saw earlier. He gave her a smile and a nod.

"Yes, Rose, I can see. It's just like I told you. He's a gentle giant."

Riley fell in love with them both. So did Merlin if the way he was sitting at Rose's feet practically begging to be petted was any indication.

"Forgive me for being so rude," Rose said as she pulled Riley into her embrace. It took Riley a second to react. It had been such a long time since anyone had given her a hug that, at first, she wasn't sure how to react. This sure wasn't the same as hugging Merlin. Riley hated to let go, but she did when Rose pulled back.

"Come in, come in, we have to get you settled."

The room was huge, and in it were four heart-backed sofas that looked as if they had come from some movie set. The room had several circular tables with what looked like fountains on them and from each fountain was a fat little cherub. If there was a bad choice that could be made in decorating a room, it had been made in here. Riley had heard the expression *a room of clichés*, but now she had seen it. She was about to comment when she turned to speak to Conner and instead saw Rose going into James's embrace.

"Welcome back, my love," Rose whispered.

"I had to come. I left my heart here," Jim said with a smile and then bent down to kiss Rose. Riley couldn't look away as the couple hugged one another. *What would that be like?* she wondered. If someone else besides Merlin was waiting for her to return home. What would it be like to have a man waiting for her? Then she lifted her gaze and found Conner looking at the couple as well, with open envy. Well, she didn't even need to ask. There was no one special in Conner's life, either.

Conner cleared his throat. "There are no guests here, so this display is just making me jealous and more determined than ever to find an older woman. If I'm lucky, I'll find my own Rose," Conner joked with James.

Rose broke away from James and pushed his hands away as she came toward Riley. "So, I heard the whole story of how you came to be here. Let me say, I'm so sorry. I'm sorry for Larry, who is a big pain in the patootie. I'm sorry for the bad roads that no one cares about until there is an accident, and most of all, I'm sorry you met Conner under such bad circumstances. He's normally a great guy and an even better boss. So, now, we'll start with the basics and get you into bed."

"The basics?" Riley asked.

Rose walked up to her and pulled her face down a couple of inches so she could kiss her cheeks. Then she took a step back and nodded at her.

"Dinner now is what I'm thinking. My mother always said, 'Kiss the boo-boos first and then feed the soul.' It's a bit brisk out, so I made some steaks for my James, but I've got plenty for us all."

Merlin came in and sat in front of Rose as if he understood what was on the menu. Rose bent down and rubbed his head.

"I've got something for you as well, old man," Rose whispered to Merlin.

"Riley, your room is the first one down the hall on your right."

"My room?" Riley said.

"Yes, I put your things in it."

She walked past him and gave him a raised eyebrow.

"A bit high handed, I think."

Conner smiled. "I'm practical. You're just upset that you agree with me."

Rose interrupted them both. "You two can bicker at the table. The steaks won't hold, so come along."

Riley went to the room to wash the smell of the hospital off of her. She rummaged through her bag and put on her vanilla sanitizer soap, and ran her wet hands through her hair, hoping to tame the wispy strands back into her pony-tail. When she had done all she had time to do, she left her room and followed the smell of steak to wind up in the kitchen.

She took a seat at the large table. It looked as if it were made from an actual tree and then glazed.

"This house has good bones," she told Conner.

Conner gave a wan smile. "You are among the minority who see the potential in this house."

"Well, it needs work, but I think you have to look at the inner beauty of an inn, not to just renovate it, but also to find out what the bestselling feature is of a place."

Merlin came in, and Rose set a bowl for him with two bones, and he laid down to begin his journey into paradise. Riley would still watch him, but the large T-bones seemed more than enough to keep Merlin occupied.

"Are you okay? I mean, really, do you feel okay?" Conner asked.

She gave him a smile and nodded. "I'm good."

"Let me know if you're dizzy or anything," he said.

Riley nodded. "You'll be the second to know."

Conner stopped and looked at her. "You know, Riley, you're a good person."

"Of course, I have a dog. That's just practical common sense. Happy dogs mean their owners are good people."

He laughed and then shook his head. "I have to fill out paperwork and make sure all is well with the hospital bill and the car claim."

"Oh, I'm sorry, you probably had some important things to do and—"

"And you came just in time to save me. I'll be back."

She watched him leave, and Rose and James sat down to eat.

"He didn't take his plate?" Riley said.

Rose waved him off. "I've known him for about ten years. Let him go do what is on his mind now, and then he will be able to focus on eating. I tell you, Conner is the reason that the creator made microwaves. He hasn't been able to sit through a whole meal yet."

It was odd the conversation went on when he left. But it gave Riley time to think. She had been so angry with Conner when she had seen his expensive-looking car. She couldn't believe how poorly she had misjudged him just based on his appearance and the way the town's people seemed to have an opinion about him too.

She must have been sitting there a bit longer than she thought because the sound of a low rumble brought her out of her thoughts. She looked on the floor and saw Merlin with his head to the side of the bowl, snoring. Riley couldn't hold back the smile.

"I hate to wake him," Riley said.

"You don't have to. It's just us three in the house. If you don't mind leaving your door cracked, I'm sure he'll be able to find you."

Riley looked at the couple and then at Merlin. This had been the reason she moved—to find nice people like Rose and James. To find a new start. It looked rocky, but after some sleep, she'd be able to figure it out. She said good night to Rose and James and looked over her shoulder in the direction that Conner went. She wouldn't bother the man. After dealing with insurance people, she would probably be his least favorite person to see right now.

She had a plan. She would get some sleep, wake up, look at the world again, and then make another attempt to make her way in her new town of Inheritance Bay.

Four

Conner was in his office when he woke to something wet on his nose. He tried to swat it away, but it wouldn't go. Again the wetness came, and this time, it was followed by puffs of hot air that left something to be desired when it came to smell. Conner opened his eyes and found himself looking into the ever-patient and expressive face of Merlin.

Well, he could affirm that he was no longer allergic to dogs. Conner looked up at the clock on the wall and realized the nap he had taken had been longer than he wanted. Rose had come in and found him, he could tell from the throw blanket across his legs. Sitting up, he rolled his shoulders and then let out a breath. He got up and went to the kitchen for dinner. The table was cleared as he expected, but on the table was a cardholder with a note.

Yours is in the microwave.

Conner smiled. He didn't know what he'd do without Rose and James sometimes. After eating his dinner, he took Merlin out to the back yard. It was enclosed, and if worse came to worse, he could stay out the night if he didn't come when he called. The backyard was straight in the back, and in the summer, they put out white iron tables with vases and flowers on them.

Conner had taken ownership of the inn about two years ago. He hadn't had time to get it ready for his parents, so it had continued to do business. Rose and James had overseen the basic running of the inn. The inn had progressed, but according to one of the reviews, it was a great place if you and your loved one wanted to entertain yourselves with your company. The food was excellent, the furniture old and cliché. Turtle doves might go to the inn, but they better have eyes only for each other if they want to enjoy it. The review had stung.

Conner wasn't good at aesthetics. He could read financials all day. He could tell you if there was money in an investment. How this investment was dressed or looked didn't factor into the equation. He wanted to make sure this place was amazing for his parents, though, so he was going to have to find a group to do the work who wouldn't sell the information to the latest newspaper.

Conner went to the door to go in, and Merlin trotted his way back. Contrary to his size, Merlin was very gentle, just like Riley had said. When they got back into the house, Conner followed Merlin as he investigated the inn. He thought he would go straight to Riley, but instead, he walked around the perimeter of the house and stopped more than once in the kitchen.

"No, old man, you need to move on. This is Rose's domain, and I like her cooking enough for us to have a serious discussion." Merlin looked over his shoulder and then moved on.

Finally, they found themselves in front of Riley's door.

"Merlin?" she called out. He knocked lightly on the door.

"It's me as well," Conner said.

"Come in, Conner."

She was sitting on the edge of the bed. Her back seemed a bit stiff.

"Is the room okay? I thought it would be best to do a room on the first floor with your injuries. The car hit your shoulder and side at a slow speed but trauma can take days not to mention the soreness and—"

She held up her hand. "I'm not one hundred percent, but I'm not ready to keel over either. Thank you for the room."

He wished there was some way he could get her to go back to the hospital. He knew the beds here were comfortable but were they made for someone with her injuries? He could tell she was sore, if nothing else. Occasionally, she shifted on the bed, and he could see the quick grimace on her face.

"I hope you find it comfy. The reviews have not been so kind," he said.

"Reviews are the best. They only say what they see today. When you finish, you'll see the true nature of the inn shine."

Well, if he were honest, Conner would admit that he wasn't sure if the inn shone at all, but he had wanted it to. He had hoped that Turtle Dove Inn would be the place he found love with Tammy.

He could have rented the inn, but he had just met Tammy. It seemed like she liked what he did and didn't mind his hours. Conner had always wanted to live in a small town and give his family the same experience his parents had done for him and his siblings. It seemed like he was on the road to having it all.

When he thought he and Tammy were going to make it, he bought the inn and several other buildings in town. He'd give this gift to his parents, and then he and Tammy would move in. He bought everything and then brought Tammy out to look at the property, and then it went downhill from there.

Maybe he had been impulsive, but that was supposed to be part of love. He wanted a place that would be theirs. He thought this town was the answer, but when Tammy arrived, she thought staying here was a joke. She explained to him that it was fine that he worked long hours because she was able to spend his money when she felt like it.

"Conner?"

He pulled himself from the past and looked at Riley. "Shine, you were saying. I don't know that I've seen that yet. I do know that when my parents come, I want it to feel like a simpler time with some amenities. I want it to feel like home and hearth. I'm hoping that I can do that."

"You may not know this, but some people think I'm stubborn. If you could get me here, then you must have a will of iron."

Conner laughed. "You win. I'll be here if you need anything?"

Riley folded her hands over her chest. "You won, and

I'm here. I'm afraid that is as far as I'm going to let this go. I have some pain killers. My body is sore by this bed feels heavenly."

"I got it. I'll see you in the morning."

Merlin curled up beside her bed, and then he backed out of the room.

Conner walked back to his office only to hear water running in the kitchen.

"You know I firmly believe you have some sort of device in the kitchen that tells you when there are dirty dishes," Conner said.

Rose waved him off. "I am just a light sleeper. When you get plates, you sound like a bull in a china shop. Is Riley settled for the night?"

"Yes, she is," he replied. "I'm just concerned that she won't say anything if she's not well. I know we are trying to get things right. I didn't mean to bring home a woman and a dog," he finished apologetically.

"Just stop it, Conner. I'm thrilled that you brought home a woman. And one that I like at that. The dog is just icing on the cake of a good thing."

Conner knew that his mother would have nothing less than what he did today. He had tried to keep those core values that had afforded him the opportunity to be more than what he was to other people. If he could, he hoped that his helping a person out when they needed it would give something back to the world for pairing him up with a family like the Sanders.

James came in through the back of the kitchen and wrapped his arms around Rose doing the dishes.

"You know I like you, Conner, but I'm keeping my

girl. These late-night meetings have got me thinking," he teased.

"You old coot. The only reason you probably got up is that your feet are cold," Rose teased back.

Conner hadn't told any of his siblings what he planned. He was sure he was going to hear it from his sisters, but he wanted to be the one to do this for his parents. He felt like he needed to in light of his failure with Tammy.

Rose cleared her throat. "You're woolgathering," she said.

Conner smiled. "I just want this to go right,"

Rose nodded. "I understand. Is there anything else you'd like us to do?"

"No, I'm going to find out what's going on with the special events company that we contracted with. They should have gotten back to me by now."

"I'm sure you'll think of something, Conner, you always do," Rose said as she and James left the kitchen.

Conner pulled out his cell phone to send a message to the company. When he saw an email from the event company, he breathed a sigh of relief. But when he opened the email, his world fell apart. The company was writing to say that due to a mix-up in names, they wouldn't be able to cover his event for his parents. They would be more than happy to give him credit for an event, and they had even added the name of a company they could recommend.

He didn't even read the name they recommended. He could just see all of his plans falling apart. It brought back Tammy's words about how he didn't fit in. He wasn't a family person, and he knew little to nothing about love. If it wasn't on a spreadsheet, he didn't understand it, and the best he could do was to buy a wife to fit in his perfect little world of family.

He could stop this now. He could just reach out to one of his siblings and tell them his idea, and they'd take care of it. His parents' anniversary was so much more important than his ego or whatever it was that made him think he could do this. Closing his eyes, he let the stress flow from him and resigned himself to doing the right thing. Then Conner opened his eyes, and sitting in front of him was Merlin.

It all started to click like a bunch of funds that should be together. He knew she was resistant to all kinds of help, but maybe if he did something for her, they could help each other, and he'd be able to live with the solution as well.

He reached down and patted Merlin on the head.

"Merlin, you may be magic after all."

Five

Riley didn't open her eyes. If she opened her eyes, Merlin would think it was time to go out. To get as much sleep as possible, she would slowly awake and keep these last moments to herself. She reached her hand out to the left and then her other hand out to the right. There was no Merlin. She was alone in her bed. Still not wanting to take a chance at having to move from her warm spot, she stretched out her legs. She felt nothing but the smooth caress of sheets beneath her legs.

Finally, she opened her eyes, and to her delight, she was all alone. Riley loved Merlin, but sometimes Merlin didn't realize how big he was or how heavy he could be. She sat up and saw her door ajar. Merlin must have gotten up already. She knew she needed to get up and tend to him, but the few moments were like gold.

To have a morning of waking up and not worrying about going to work, a grouchy landlord, or even worse, a friend who was telling her to be quiet and hide outside with Merlin until their landlord or parent left. To wake up, worry-free was a luxury.

As she scooted to the side of the bed and put her feet over the side, every place where her back had connected with the sidewalk yesterday made itself known. Her gaze quickly went to the door, and she sat stock still, hoping no one would come by to wish her good morning or bring news of Merlin. She needed to get her game face together if she was going to hide today's surprises. Fortunately, she had some pain killers, but with the way she was hurting, it felt like the pills would only dull the pain that was already coursing through her whole body.

Finding a job and place was hard enough. Telling someone she was hurt would scare away most people. She was a stranger in town, and sympathy only went so far. When Marjorie saw her, what would she think? Riley had to get dressed. She bet that Conner was one of those type-A personalities who were ahead of the game and on the move. He probably met Merlin this morning to go on the morning walk.

She slipped out of bed and thought it was worse than the first day of her cramps. She had only fallen to the ground, not down a flight of steps. Gritting her teeth, she pushed forward and found some clothing in her bags. She found a pair of jeans and a blue t-shirt. It took all of her energy to get those on. By the time she was done, the pain was at a low throb.

She was sure she could make it if she took very small steps and no deep breaths. Riley left her room and then went back out to the common area and took a seat on a heart-backed sofa. It wasn't a bad sofa. It was comfy at the very least. She supposed the décor wasn't too bad once you got used to it, but she could feel a creative itch beginning. She thought of things she could suggest to make not just the room but the whole inn pop. It had such a homey potential about it, but it was wasted on tacky commercialism.

She could see why Conner had bought the place. Even with the cheesy décor, it was still making money. Going to bed and breakfasts or places removed from the city was popular. Riley wondered if by closing it now, he would lose money. It didn't seem like money was an issue for him, but she supposed Rich people got rich by holding on to their money.

As if thinking about the man had summoned him, he walked by the door with Merlin on a homemade leash. It was one of those thin, retractable leashes. Merlin must have liked him because he could break away from one of those leashes without trying too hard.

Conner had on a blue turtleneck and blue jeans. He looked alert but distracted. His hair was windblown and called to her to run her hands through it. She had to tear her gaze away from him.

She had just met Conner. True, she was already calling him by his first name, and she had stayed the night in his house. She took a breath and reminded herself that they didn't live in the same circles. She wasn't a classist, but she had just arrived at Inheritance. It was perfectly normal to be attracted to a man who had a competent air about him, strong shoulders, and brown eyes that made you listen to every word that came out of his mouth. She shook her head and saw that Merlin had seen her. She had to get a grip. The fact that she was attracted to Conner so soon was just a sign that she had been around Merlin too long and not enough men. Really the first one that shows up she likes, what was she thinking?

"Conner," she said as she raised her arm. She clenched her jaw with the movement.

"I didn't see you. I was going to make you some breakfast and come get you. Are you hungry?" he asked.

She shook her head no. *Great, and he cooks.*

"I don't usually eat breakfast. My jobs usually have me up so early that it's too early to eat, so I make sure to have lunch."

He unleashed Merlin, who came over and lay down next to her feet, and then Conner sat down on the couch. Riley wanted to ask why he was stopping, certainly, he had other people to dazzle with his charm and consideration.

"So, how are you feeling?" he asked.

"I've been better. It's not the worst, but I've definitely been better."

"Wow, that was a vague answer. When I get those answers, it usually means the worst. So I take it you are in a lot of pain," he said sympathetically.

Riley held up her hand. "Listen, I'm not saying I'm going to be running anywhere soon, but I can move about and do work. It's my side that took the brunt of it. As long as I don't stretch, I'm good."

"Good, Good," he said, and then they both lapsed into silence.

When it got a bit, awkward Riley broke it. "So, it seems like you are a bigwig in town. You paid for my hospital stay. Your business isn't here in Inheritance, is it?"

He smiled. "No, I own a company called Wealth Builders. We—"

"You manage portfolios and make a lot of people big money. I know the company. So, you are *the* Conner Sanders?"

"I am."

"So you can run your company from here?"

"Kind of. I have good people. I worked hard to find people so I wouldn't work all the time."

"So I've got to ask. You could have obviously paid to get things here in the B and B done. What gives? Are you going into B and Bs?"

He relaxed on the couch, extending his legs. Who knew that the finance genius had such muscular legs? Riley had to look at Merlin, hoping Conner didn't notice her checking him out.

"I'm sure I told you, or you heard. My parents are coming here for their anniversary, and I wanted to make it special. My siblings will be coming as well, and I wanted to do something for all of them."

"All of them? You say it like it's the horde," she joked.

"Well, I'm adopted, but I'm the last adoptee. My parents adopted six before me."

"I can't imagine that, being an only child."

"Well, you can more than imagine it. My family will be here soon."

"I'm sure I'll be gone by then."

"I'm actually hoping that's not true. I had a horrible thing happen last night, and then Merlin helped me to see that it could be a great thing," Conner said. He looked like a boy who had just gotten a train for Christmas.

"I have to tell you I'm highly suspicious of a plan that is inspired by Merlin, whose favorite past time is to lay about," Riley jokes.

"I'd like to pitch it."

"Go for it."

"I want to know if you'll work for me," Conner asked.

Riley looked at Conner and then at Merlin.

"Stop looking to Merlin. He is not helping you in the least," Riley said.

"No, wait, let me say this right. You know, this is why I have a department that does presentations," he laughed. "You see, I did hire some help to fix the place up, and they sent me an email last night canceling. I need help. My family will be here in a week and a half. I know you came to do an apprenticeship of sorts. It was probably going to be with Larry, and I don't think that will fit either one of you. So what do you think?"

"I think you are a desperate man, but doing this could be a fiasco. I have worked in other hotels, but this isn't just a hotel thing; this is for your family, and I'm not sure I know enough about them to do this."

"Okay, what do you want to know?" he asked.

"No, Conner, it's not that easy. I mean, I'm sure they are used to fancier stuff than what I know and—"

"Are you saying we're snobs?"

"No! I'm saying that they may have a baseline expectation that I don't know how to—"

"Conner, I hate to be so personal but don't you have a woman who can assist with this?" Riley asked. She didn't want to ask it, but she had to, for all sorts of reasons, and unfortunately, the most crucial reason she needed the answer had everything to do with her personally.

"I had one at one point, but let's say that things didn't work out the way I thought they would. To be honest, I thought there was going to be someone to do this with me, but like I said, it didn't go right. So Rose and James traveled with me, and they have been doing their best to help out. My family isn't going to need someone to cook and clean for them. I just want to make sure all of their needs are met while they are here. I need you to run the house while they're here. I have the services that come to the inn regularly. I want to make it special, and I need someone not from town to help me out. Will you help me, Riley? I need you."

Riley was so happy that her hand was on Merlin's head. Otherwise, it would have gone straight to her mouth. Did this man know he looked great, and him saying those words made him a knight without armor?

"Conner, I don't know. It seems like you might need more time to think this through."

"On the contrary, I have been thinking it through. I even wrote up a chart to make sure I had all the pros and cons."

"You made a chart?"

"Yes, I usually do a chart for everything. This was important, so I did one."

"Ah, so what did the chart tell you?"

Conner smiled. The man had no clue what his smile did for his face. It took him from attractively brooding to a friendly boyfriend.

"The chart told me that you would make the perfect hostess. I like you. I can trust you. You could have asked for a ton of money, and I would have paid it. You didn't.

You made sure I took care of your dog. It says you are responsible, and the fact that Merlin is old says you are compassionate. I know you can do this if only you wanted to help me out."

Riley was confused and happy all at the same time. She could do this. It wasn't charity; he needed help. She could use this time to get the lay of the land in this town. She would have good experience from a high profile name if it went south. Right now, the most important thing was he was willing to let Merlin stay as well.

"How will we work out the pay? I was told there would be a stipend and—"

"I'll pay you a fair wage, and you'll stay here. For the number of people coming and being on call 24/7, I couldn't pay you a stipend it wouldn't be fair for what I'm expecting. You will be earning your keep, so to speak."

In the back of her mind, she thought this was a made-up job. She would've given it more credence if the first company hadn't canceled. Being who he was, Conner could get another company that would try to move heaven and earth to do this for him. She was picking things apart again. She was still confused.

"Listen, I can't expect you to make these kinds of decisions right away. Why don't we talk about it later today? I just want it to germinate in your mind for a bit. Imagine working in this place where you could put your mark on it. Staying in this Valentine haven and making it the ultimate Valentine for a couple that deserves the best."

"I'm glad you're not pushing it, and yes, it's very apparent why you have a sales department. This presentation was a bit…"

"A bit?"

"I'm not one to criticize, especially as it's in my favor, but you shouldn't leave that CEO office too soon if I were you," she said with a smile.

He got up from the sofa and smiled back at her.

"I'm leaving so you can come to the right decision."

"Real subtle, Conner. Off with you," Riley said, laughing as he kept looking over his shoulder, winking at her.

When he was gone, and just Merlin was left, she closed her eyes and tried to clear her mind. She had heard other women say how smart guys were so attractive, and now here she was with Mr. Rich-and-Geeky, and he was getting her attention in new ways. She had to pull herself together. He wanted a hostess, not a girlfriend. It seemed as though he didn't have either one of those, though.

Riley patted her lap, and Merlin stood up and placed his head on her knee. Besides, the real question wasn't if he was interested in her. Was she interested in him?

"Come on, Merlin, you are about to have a banner day. I need to walk some of this stiffness out while I think about our future and if it involves a man who likes lists."

Six

What had she been thinking, taking that walk with Merlin? Trying to keep up with him had been its own form of torture. She had made it back to the inn, but now she was sitting at the kitchen table. She had to get Merlin some water. She would just rest a moment and then crawl back to her room.

"I see you're ready for lunch," Rose said.

Riley's eyes popped open, and she plastered a smile on her face. "I've been out with Merlin, so I wouldn't be opposed," she said.

"No worries, I was just seeing when you had some interest. Conner said it's your first big meal of the day."

"Did he now?" Riley murmured. "I didn't see him around."

"Oh Conner and James are in the back. Conner is helping James carve out wooden nameplates for everyone."

Riley thought about Conner making nameplates and

the first image that came to mind is him making a list on what would be the best way to go about it.

"I can tell what you're thinking, Riley," Rose said. "I know that Conner doesn't seem like the physical type, but for people he loves, he'll go out of his norm to make them happy. It's what makes him the best of people to work for."

Then Rose brought out a plate with burgers and sourdough bread. Riley could see four patties and fries on the side. She looked at the plates and the condiments on the side.

"Rose, are you eating with me?"

"I'll eat a bite with you while the men are out, but most of it is for you. Conner said you needed to build your strength and start out right."

Riley looked at the plates she was bringing out, and then Rose sat down. When Rose passed out the plates, she gave Riley a dish and then put a saucer in front of herself.

"Rose?" Riley asked, looking at the saucer.

"I just don't eat that much, but I love to watch others eat my food. So eat up," Rose said with a laugh.

Riley made a burger while Rose pecked at the fries.

"So Conner hinted you might be staying on."

"He hinted? Somehow I don't think Conner knows how to hint at anything."

"I think it would be great if you stayed. His family is coming, and he wants to make this so special for his parents. When that money-grubbing snake, Tammy, left she did it to leave him in a lurch and the threats she sent to him as well."

"Threats?"

Rose shook her head. "We aren't supposed to talk about that. We're sure he can handle any threat that came up," Rose said.

Threats? Riley thought about the girlfriend. She hadn't really asked the status of his ex or why they had broken up. Then the words Conner said to her came back with a vengeance. He had said he knew he could trust her because she could have asked for any amount of money, and he would have paid it.

"Conner loves his parents," Rose said. "The Sanders didn't have money growing up. In fact, they took on the kids when they were comfortable and could have traveled the world, but instead, they took on new kids who they thought needed them."

Riley wanted to ask if his parents knew about the threats and if she could get some more details on the threat, but she had a feeling Rose had said all she was going to about the subject for the day.

"They sound like amazing people."

"They are and not a mean bone in their bodies."

"I hope you're right. If they are, then my job becomes ten times easier," Riley said.

Rose nodded. "So you've decided on taking the job?"

Riley was hesitant but couldn't see a problem. When all else failed, she would trust Merlin's opinion every time. Merlin liked it here, and he liked the people. She knew she wouldn't find a better offer. Just when she was about to question Rose some more, he came into the kitchen.

He was dressed in a running suit. His hair was flat on his head with sweat, and he was out of breath, making his chest inflate like a well-chiseled bellows. Looking at him, Riley laughed to herself then. Conner Sanders sweated like everyone else. He was an ordinary, considerate, gorgeous guy who had money. He looked to Riley and had the beginning of a burgeoning smile on his face.

"Are you going to take the job?" he asked.

Her pride was warring with her inner woman. Her pride said she and Merlin had made it this far, and they didn't need Conner. Then there was the woman inside of her that said it would be nice to play hostess/woman of the house for a bit. She could fix up the inn and clock some serious experience.

"Yes, I was so blown away by your subtle petition that I had to say yes."

Riley looked at Conner and could see he was entirely too pleased with himself. He had to know that he would win.

"There are some formalities to address, and then we can decide when you'll start."

"Instead of our lack of time and how much work is required, I think we should do the formalities while I get started."

"I know there are some things to do, but it is a functioning inn. How much do you think needs to be done?"

Riley looked around and then looked back at Conner.

"A person can be breathing, but it doesn't mean that they are in the best condition, does it?"

"Wow, just breathing! That's a pretty low bar."

Riley went to stand in front of him and then said in a low voice so that only he could hear.

"If you aren't sure how dire the situation is, ask

yourself where you last saw cherubs on pedestals inside of a building, and then let me know when you come up with somewhere besides a mausoleum."

"I'll get on it right away," Conner said as he excused himself from the room. Riley had to keep the smile to herself. Conner might be a rich financial genius, but it seemed like he had a thing or two to learn about mood, atmosphere, and love. Love? Riley tried to clear her head. She was going to help Conner out and get herself set up in her new town. She wasn't looking for love, and even if she were, she and Conner couldn't be more different.

"Any news?" Conner asked his lawyer.

"We are still in negotiations. She's saying that there was a verbal."

Conner let his head fall back against the headrest in his office.

"Have we all agreed on the gag order?"

"Her lawyers are saying it's as good as the rest of the deal," Conner let out a sigh. "Keep me abreast. If it turns out that the situation changes, let me know.

Conner hung up the phone with the head of Wealth Builders' legal team and tried to pry his mind away from the potential problem he hoped they would be able to resolve. Rose had furnished this room for him. At first, he didn't think he had a preference, but she had been with him long enough that this office looked like every office he had off-site of Wealth Builders. When he asked her about it, she told him she wanted him to be comfortable no matter where he was.

It wasn't long before the door to his office opened, and Rose came in. It was only a matter of time before she would come and check on him anyway. He waited for her to speak, but as usual, he was always the first one to break the silence.

"Can you provide Riley with all of the contacts we have to get the inn ready?"

"I've already given them to her," she said calmly. "She's already started to call people to see who's available and what is available."

"Thank you, Rose. How about you and James? It's not too late if you want to go somewhere else for the week of Valentine's Day."

"We have each other, Conner. According to James, every day is Valentine's Day," Rose said. "Now stop trying to avoid the issue. How is the matter with Tammy coming along?"

He wanted to be able to block out the problem as easily as he had closed his eyes. "It's still in play," he said.

"Has she come up with new demands or at least a dollar amount?"

"No dollar amount. The team thinks she's waiting until Valentine's Day to threaten to release her claims for the maximum benefit and maximum sympathy."

"Your gut feeling?"

"She's holding out for the biggest cash reward." The words were monotone as they left Conner's mouth. His hand reflexively went to his left hand, where he had tried on rings with Tammy at a very exclusive jeweler. Now pictures of those moments were being held over his head with a price tag that she wouldn't disclose.

What would he be able to tell his family if she went through with her threat and told everyone that he had tried to buy her with gifts to show up at the inn and pretend to be the perfect couple for his parents' anniversary? His family had done so much for him that this would be an emotional blow to his parents. His siblings would survive, but the fact that he might be the cause of any discomfort for his parents tore him up in new ways.

"And since you know this, why didn't you offer an amount?"

"If we offer an amount, that will be the starting point for her asking," he answered Rose. As the words left him, he felt dirty and trapped. He wanted to ignore her. His company wouldn't be hurt by her claims, but Tammy had done her homework well. She had found the one thing that he would protect no matter what, his family.

"This isn't your fault," she said.

Rose had told him that same thing more than once, and he still hadn't been able to accept it.

"I know it's not my fault."

Rose laughed. "I think you should leave lying to someone else as well. You are terrible at it."

"Maybe I'm fine, and you are just super sensitive to me. Anyway, it doesn't matter. I can't control it either way right now, so we need to let it go and try to make the best of the week when they are here."

"Are you happy with Riley?" Rose asked.

Was he happy? It was an odd question. What he could say was he was comfortable around her. She was fiercely independent, and it called to him like he never thought it would.

"Riley is an honest person who loves her dog and isn't afraid to take chances, just like she did to come to Inheritance Bay."

"Do you think she can manage to get the inn up to snuff and make your family feel at home?"

"I'm not worried about her being able to do what she says."

He heard Rose stand up. "Well, then my job is done. I'll leave you to finish up what you need for the day, but don't stay in here so long that I have to come and get you."

When the door closed, he pulled himself to the desk, turned on both desk monitors, and then turned on some classical music as he began to work. Spreadsheets, emails, and project plans. All of them flowed over the screens as the music played. Here he could get lost. Here was where he was the most comfortable.

He thought last year that he had it all when Tammy seemed to accept his lifestyle. Now he was going to pay for his arrogance. The worst of it was that his family would pay with him.

Conner didn't know how much time had passed, but his music had stopped when he felt a hard tapping on his leg. He looked down to see Merlin's tail wagging and hitting his calf as he looked at the door. As if he were guarding him.

"Hey, guy."

When he spoke, Merlin turned to him and jumped up until his paws were on the chair's armrest.

"I think you are a bit big for that. However, good thing you came in. I don't think I want Rose to hunt me down twice today."

He walked out of his office to find that everyone and heard voices coming from the main entrance to the inn.

Riley was talking to some workers they kept on hand for the inn. She was directing them to change out the cherub stands for water fountains. There were several rugs rolled up on the sides and pillows on the couch. He hadn't thought about it, but the pillows were probably a good idea. He certainly couldn't sit for a long time on those sofas.

He watched her explain the changes and things she wanted, and the contractor followed behind her, writing rapidly and nodding his head. She needed to rest. Every so often, when she moved from one side of the room to show the contractor one point or another, he would see a slight grimace before she covered it up with a smile.

He wanted to say he was watching Riley just to make sure her health was okay, but Conner didn't lie to himself. As she stretched and pointed to things, he could tell she was a fit woman with just the right amount of curves. She wasn't curvaceous, but she was just right. Then, as if she could tell where his thoughts were going, both she and the contractor stopped and looked at him.

"Conner, I hope you don't mind, we needed to start right away, and Rose gave me all of the information."

He tried to hear the words she was saying and not the husky tones she spoke in. "I need to make sure you are taking care of yourself," he warned.

"I hear you," she said and then turned to go back to the contractor.

He smiled then. He was sure she heard him but whether or not she listened was the real question. How could he complain to her about health? He hadn't listened to a soul when they said he needed time away from the company. The only holidays he took were his family member's birthdays and anniversaries.

Conner looked at her going strong, and he had an idea. He went to the kitchen and cut them both apple pie and heated it up in the microwave. He found some fresh cream in the refrigerator and put a couple of dollops on top. By the time he made it to the common area, the contractor was gone, and Riley was standing looking about the room. When he cleared his throat, she gave him a confused look. When she saw the tray in his hands, her face went from surprise to skepticism. What made an attractive woman have that look? Rose had asked if Riley made him happy, but he could see now that he hadn't asked enough questions about Riley to find out if she was happy or, more importantly, what was it that made coming to a brand new place and leaving all you knew a viable option.

"I was hoping we could have some pie together?"

She shrugged and took a seat on the sofa. "I can take a moment, but looking at the size of that pie, I don't think I can eat a whole piece."

"Was that David from the antique store?" he asked.

She looked at him in surprise. "Yes, it was. He said that a lot of the furniture came from there."

"That explains why he knows so much when I tell him we have an issue," Conner smiled.

"Well, he's going to move some furniture and give us some sofas that are regular. He owns the furniture store as well, so we may be able to get some show-floor pieces at a steal. He said he'd send me pics and whatever I liked he would bring."

"Wow, you're good. I had a lot more challenges getting deliveries out here."

"Well, when he first started, I could see he wanted to haggle. I'm okay with haggling, so it wasn't so bad."

He watched her take a bite of her apple pie and realized that he was entranced by the way her lips closed over the fork and her eyes closed as she savored the bite.

"This pie is amazing!"

No, she was the amazing one here. What was he thinking? Riley was an attractive woman, not the next Helen of Troy, but she had her own charm and beauty. Hadn't he learned anything from Tammy? He wasn't very good at choosing when it came to women.

On the eve of finding out if one woman would ruin his parents' anniversary was not the best time to be looking at another woman in a romantic way. They weren't so much alike. He just needed to focus on the differences.

"I don't like haggling," he said firmly.

"I find that hard to believe," she said.

"What? I work with finances and other people's wealth."

Riley smiled. "I guess that means that everyone gives you the price you want on the first go-round?"

"Well, no, sometimes we have to review it to see what it's really worth, and then—"

"You mean you haggle about the price?"

He stopped and thought about it. Conner could see the triumphant look on her face. "Okay, so I might do some form of haggling. However, I want you to know, that you don't need to haggle for anything. I can't think of a thing you'd want for this coming event that we couldn't get you."

Conner thought about how he had all but opened his wallet to her. What was it? Was it because he liked her on so many levels that he was willing to trust his feelings around her?

She held up her hand.

"Thank you for giving me the keys to the kingdom, but I won't need them. Like I said before, the changes that need to be made are small," Riley said.

They ate the pie and said nothing. It wasn't rushed or awkward, and Conner was once again taken back. He didn't have to do anything. There was a calmness sitting here with Riley that was sweet. It seeped through his bones and made him toasty inside. When he was done eating, he almost regretted it. Conner looked next to him and found Riley looking at him as well.

"Thank you, Riley," he said, reaching out to take her plate.

She nodded and gave him a shy smile. He rose to walk away, baffled by the feeling but not wanting to push or rush Riley. He tried not to let the feeling of disappointment flood him as he stood up.

"Umm, Conner?" Riley said.

Conner tensed at hearing his name. "Yeah?"

"Hold up, I'll come with you to the kitchen. We can clean up so Rose doesn't have to." She said.

In truth, it didn't matter what Riley said. What mattered to Conner was he was going to have more time with her.

"Okay, I'll keep you company."

Seven

For a moment, he thought she wasn't coming into the kitchen. He had gathered up all of the dishes and was debating whether to put them in a dishwasher or do them by hand. He wasn't too good for it; he'd washed a dish or two in his day. Admittedly it had been an industrial one, but he knew the mechanics. Today he'd be reliving those moments to spend more time with Riley.

"Are you really about to wash dishes?" she asked.

"I do know how to wash dishes. I want you to know I consider the basic utilities in an apartment or coop to be a dishwasher, but I can live without one. Besides, why start up the machine for four items?"

He hoped he sounded more confident than he felt. He grabbed the sponge and squeezed the dishwashing liquid onto it.

"Aren't you going to wet the sponge first?" she asked.

"No, it's a sponge. When it's dry and open, the soap can get in the sponge, so I only have to soap it once," he replied. She shook her head, but she didn't look like she was on board with the theory. At this point, he wasn't on board with the theory.

"So have you always gone all out for their anniversary?"

"It's always been celebrated as if it were Christmas." Conner thought of the planning that would happen around his parents' anniversary and how everyone would find a gift, either store-bought, handmade, or regifted sometimes. His parents' anniversary was the crux of why they were all there. His parents used to just have a small dinner when the kids were small.

His mother would say that their anniversary was the day they decided to adopt. They always met up and had dinner with everyone. No matter where the kids were or what they were doing, everyone would come home for that anniversary dinner. His mom had told him it wasn't just a celebration of their wedding; it was the day the idea of a family had been born.

"When I was growing up, our mom explained that their anniversary was the birthday of our family, and who didn't want to have two birthdays?" he said. "The gifts were things you were grateful for. So more than once, I got a calculator or green bar paper. Everyone was grateful I knew how to manipulate numbers. One of the things we would argue over was who got to sit the closest to Mom and Dad. I would always lose because my dad would say men shouldn't fight with women, and I had one brother and five sisters."

Riley laughed as he told the story. "I guess that meant you could only fight with your brother then?"

"It's true, Andrew and I were allowed to fight with each other, but he was the first one and oldest, so I had to outthink him if I wanted to get his spot. My oldest sisters, Grace and Aria, had an agreement, and they never fought over their spots. The middle sisters are twins, Stella and Willow, would do just as you, haggle to get the best spot. And the youngest girl in the family perfected tears. It didn't get Piper everything, but it sure did help with a lot."

Conner smiled when he thought about how they grew up and how lucky they had all been to be adopted. So many children weren't.

"Your mom sounds amazing."

Conner turned on the water and started to scrub the plates with a smile.

"She is the most loving person I know. Whenever any of us told her we had a dream to do something, she supported it. She made each one of us feel like we were her favorite and chosen child close to her heart."

"Your family is still close-knit now that you've all grown up?"

"We are," he said as she rinsed the saucer. When Conner had gone to go college, he thought he would have been outed as an orphan. He thought everyone would know he was adopted because there would be something that "real" families did that he hadn't done. Instead, he found people on campus jealous about the relationship he had with his family. It was when he discovered how fortunate he was that he decided to make it on his own.

In the early days, he had something to prove. He wanted to make sure they all knew that he hadn't been a mistake. He also wanted to show the other families that had passed him up or given him back that they had made a mistake.

"Your family?" he asked, trying not to reflect on how he'd had so much to prove when it hadn't been true. It had been his insecurity running amok.

"I'm an only child. My mother passed early, leaving my father like a lost rudder. My father worked very hard not to be home or around me. I'm told I look a lot like my mother, and I suppose that played into it. It made for interesting times and a strained relationship."

Conner was at a loss for words. He thought his situation was complicated, but he couldn't imagine not having his siblings and his parents. Again, Riley was proving to be a stronger person than most. For someone who didn't seem like they had gotten a lot of the affection that he had taken for granted, she was still kind and compassionate.

"My brother says I need to look at the big picture and that I don't because I'm so focused on the problem at hand. I didn't even ask you if you wanted to stay in Inheritance Bay. I mean, for all I know, you had a job waiting for you or one you could have gone back to."

She shook her head. "My old job was getting old in a lot of ways. If I went back there, I would have to address a lot of issues that I don't want to deal with."

"Issues with employers never bode well, but I can't imagine what the issue would be with you. I think you have a great temperament. I mean, I hit you with my car, and you fix my inn. What was the issue, if you don't mind me asking?"

"My boss really was happy with my job performance. H-he just thought that since we seemed to suit so well on the job, we would suit well together personally."

He scrubbed the clean plate and then rinsed them both off. Why hadn't he asked what happened before? Here he was making sure she wasn't like Tammy, and he wasn't going to get taken for a ride again, and she had just left an uncomfortable situation with a former employer.

"I started at the restaurant because it was attached to a bed and breakfast. I didn't have the kitchen experience, and my goal was to work in every section. My boss indulged me and let me in the kitchen, and in two years, I was running the kitchen. Then he started with the hints that he had given me my chance and that I owed him."

Conner looked around the counter and realized he had no place to put the dishes. He opened up the dishwasher and placed the clean plates in the rack to dry. He needed to do something as he thought over what Riley was saying. She had no family and no job prospects to go to, through no fault of her own. To boot, he had tapped her with his car when she came to town to start over. He couldn't imagine her life or how she stayed so upbeat and positive.

"Stop thinking that hard over there, Conner," she said. "I'm not some poor, lost waif who needs to be saved or who can't look out for herself. It's true, I don't have the normal family or relationship attachments, but I have friends I can call on if I need to and a great dog to keep me company."

"I don't think *poor Riley*. What I'm thinking is you are way stronger than anyone I've ever met."

Riley looked at him and smiled. Those brown-silk eyes glimmered with pride and admiration. Not wanting to embarrass her, he looked around the kitchen and saw Merlin asleep on the floor.

"He sure gets around," Conner said, nodding towards Merlin. "What made you name him Merlin?"

Riley chuckled lightly. "That ability he has to just move from room to room without anyone noticing it? When my girlfriend had him in foster care, we thought it was magic, and so we named him Merlin."

"Well, it seems you named him aptly. I want to thank you, Riley. You've jumped in, and Rose says you've got this all under control."

"I do. Like I said, every hotel or inn has its own charm. You just need to find it and highlight it."

Well, I'm happy you've found the true face of the inn, but I don't want you to work and not play. So I'm willing to offer a compromise that I think we will both enjoy."

"You know you do a lot of haggling for a man who doesn't haggle," she teased.

Conner scratched his head. "You know, you're right. I've been thinking about that as well but what I meant to say is that tomorrow I'm going to have some horses brought to the inn. We've set up one of the two-car garages as a place to store the animals. I thought you'd like to go with me to see the horses."

"I don't know, Conner, maybe I shouldn't—"

"The guests will use it. I just want you to try it first."

He saw her trying to find a way out of it, and when she couldn't, he could see the acceptance on her face.

"Okay, I'll meet you here tomorrow.

"Great, it's a date."

"A professional meet," she said.

He nodded. "Very professional. We will be testing out the horse-drawn carriage for two," he said with a smile.

"Oh, I think you would be very dangerous at the market. Hagglers wouldn't know what to do with you," Riley said. "Fine, I'll see you tomorrow."

After she left the kitchen, Conner felt like he had just gotten off of a roller coaster. In his eighteen-year-old ignorance, his dad had once told him that this was what love felt like. The only thing that had ever given him that feeling was numbers. Today he watched a woman walk out of his kitchen who could make him feel like he did when he was with his numbers.

Eight

What had she been thinking when she agreed to go out on this "date"? Riley met him in the kitchen, figuring other people would be in the kitchen for lunch or, at the very least, going through the kitchen.

"Glad to see you are looking cheerful this afternoon. I saw you coming from your office. I assume business is good?"

Conner gave her a smile, and if she hadn't been leaning against the wall waiting, it would have knocked her off of her feet. What was it about him that as soon as he relaxed, he started to look more and more like a top model?

"I'm working on something that is going well, thank you for asking. And how about you? Part of today is to make sure you are actually taking it easy."

Riley didn't know how to answer that one without sending off all of his alarm bells. She was achy, but she had been worse. She had still taken the pills, but she definitely took less today than yesterday. Going on the morning walks was all the therapy she needed. Walking for an hour three times a day would work out most kinks.

"I'm not like the day the warranty was put out, but I'm good," she said.

"I'm glad to hear it." Then he did it again. He smiled at her, and any moment, she was expecting that twinkle to sparkle from his teeth.

"The horses were brought this morning. It's my understanding they have spent the morning adjusting to the garage and meeting Merlin. So shall we go see what condition they are in?"

She wanted to say no. But how did one tell her boss, Listen, I don't really want to hang around you too much because you are totally my type, and I feel as though I might be focusing on you more than I am focusing on doing a good job?

"Let's go look." Riley donned the heavy sweater she had brought for the occasion. Merlin walked with them out the front door so they could walk around the property. There was no access to the garages through the back yard of the inn. So when the lucky couple came for their ride, the horses would have to be brought to the front, or they would have to walk to the back of the inn.

Riley was a little nervous. He had been in his office all day, so she wasn't even sure he would notice the small touches she had put in the main area. When they walked in, he stopped in the middle of the room and looked around. Okay, he noticed.

Where the cherubs had been, there were delicate water fountains, and on the walls were framed pictures of his family. On the back wall and the archway over the door were blown-up pictures from other anniversary parties they had thrown for his parents.

"How and when did you do this?" he asked.

"Do you like it? If you don't, I can take it down, but I was so moved by your stories, and you had said that this is like your Christmas. I've heard families reminisce at Christmas, so I thought you'd like to do the same."

He walked up to her and picked up both of her hands in his, and brought them to his lips.

"Thank you, Riley. I don't know when you had time, but this means a lot to me."

Riley wanted to make him happy, and now that she knew he was, there was a feeling of warmth and accomplishment that made her feel like she had just conquered a big hill.

"I told you I wanted to make this special for you and your family."

"I have to ask; how did you get the pictures?"

"Rose helped me out," Riley confessed. In truth, Riley would have told him anything he wanted to know as long as he was holding on to her hands. She was just trying to think cool thoughts so she wouldn't sweat while he was holding her hand.

"Again, thank you. Now let's see if I can do as good a job as you did," Conner said, dropping her hands and walking towards the door. When the front door opened, Riley welcomed it. She just hoped her face wasn't red as a tomato.

When they walked outside, the air was cool and crisp. The sunlight illuminated the ground, but it did little to actually heat anything. Still, there were things that Riley still loved about the place. She loved being able to come out and not hear the hustle and bustle of cars. One of the things she wanted to be able to do in her new home was to hear her thoughts. Riley thought if she had been able to hear her thoughts earlier, she would have left earlier and found herself a better place for her and Merlin.

She wasn't a country girl, but the retrofit they did on the garage made it look like there had always been two stalls here for the horses. Piles of hay were on the ground. Riley couldn't even see the cement that she knew was under there.

Merlin walked in and found a mound of hay and lay down on it. He looked as if he had always been there. The walls were lined with hooks that held all sorts of equipment. She could only identify the halter that went around the horses and some blankets, but the layout was meticulous and even. An older man was in the garage, talking in low tones to one horse as he brushed it down. The horses looked ginormous.

Riley was a city girl, and horses looked cute on television. Now that she was here in front of not one but two, she had a newfound appreciation for them. They were a red-brown that glowed from the man's ministrations. However, the horses themselves were massive and muscular. She had watched all of the popular vet shows. Now that she was really looking at a horse, she had way more respect for those veterinarians.

When the man was done talking, he looked up and gave Riley a smile. Then he walked right up to her with a leather strap in hand, bringing the beautiful giant with him. Riley stepped back straight into a chest. Arms went around her, and she could hear Conner speaking next to her ear.

"I've got you, Riley. The horse won't hurt you. We've got two horses that work with people who have a phobia of horses, so they are very patient and calm."

In that moment, Riley's senses were confused. She wanted to run from the beast in front of her, but she wanted to snuggle into the warm body behind her.

"Riley, I want you to meet Jamie. He came with the horses," Conner said with a laugh.

The older man waved Conner off. "Conner is being modest. I was hopeless with nothing to do in my life when Conner was kind enough to give this old man some purpose by giving me this job. I've always been around horses, and I love introducing them to other people.

"This one's name is Samson," Jamie said. "He's stable and won't scare. He's pulled carriages, been around dogs and other farm animals. Loud noises don't bother him, and neither do children's squeals. He's a steady lad."

Riley heard Jamie speak with gratefulness in his tone, and it softened her heart for Conner. He had bought a horse so his parents could have this buggy ride, and he had been aware enough to give an old man some purpose. Oh yeah, she could firmly say that her boss was a sweet man.

It was so hard to reconcile this vision of Conner with the things she had heard in town. A lot of people just knew him as the man who had bought a third of it. To hear the town, talk about him, he was an unfeeling mogul who had swooped down on a town that was vulnerable. None of those things lined up with what she knew about Conner.

She knew he was a wealthy businessman, and certainly he had to make some decisions that put money first. Riley understood that but still couldn't see Conner doing something that would hurt others deliberately.

She must have been taking too long because Samson took a step towards her and nudged her shoulder. At first, she was sure he was going to take a bite out of her, but when she felt the colossal head rub up against her, she was pleasantly surprised. When Samson stepped back, he looked at Riley as if waiting for her to make a move.

"Look, Riley, Samson likes you, and you didn't have to bring carrots like I did. He obviously has good taste."

That man! Here she was trying to decide if she trusted Samson, and he was throwing around comments like that. The kind of comments that made her insides melt.

"Jamie, I'd like to take a look at Sugar."

Jamie nodded. As soon as Conner had moved, the warmth started to leave her back, and her faculties returned.

"Sugar?" Riley asked.

Jamie smiled. "That horse has a sweet nature, and he loves sugar cubes. He was a rescue and never a peep out of him. Samson will take you out of the rain, but Sugar will stay with you in a storm and never leave your side."

Conner checked on Sugar, and Riley worked up enough courage to brush Samson. *If only everything else were this simple*, Riley thought as she stood next to the behemoth.

Nine

Now Jamie knew he was interested in Riley thought Conner. There was nothing to check on Sugar. Conner just needed to put space between him and Riley. What had he been thinking standing that close to Riley? When she bumped into him, it was like a cloud of femininity had formed around them both and put him under a spell that he willingly entered. To not make a fool of himself and throw himself at her feet, he had to move.

Maybe the issue was he was feeling more since his family was coming. When he looked at Riley, he wished she wasn't everything he admired in a woman. It was true that Riley was a physically attractive woman, but it was the things you couldn't see that appealed to him the most.

She made him want to be a hero and save her and give her all the Merlins she wanted. She made him laugh and appreciate how much he had and how fortunate he was to have a family. She made him want to try to trust a woman again. Here he was not even done with Tammy, and Riley made him hope again.

Tammy had given him all the warning signs, but he had ignored them. She had wanted the best jewelry. She needed to be with the people who made the cover of magazines regardless if he was there or not. Tammy was an attractive woman, but she had told him the truth when they broke up. She had said a woman like her only had youth for so long, and she needed to capitalize on it while the iron was hot. He couldn't even imagine Riley having that thought.

Riley was a private woman who had too much pride for her own good. She was exactly what he saw, and Conner had to admit he liked what he saw. It was insane to fall for any woman when his last one was trying to blackmail him.

After stalling for another five minutes, Conner suggested they go back inside. The silence between them was welcome and not awkward. Another thing that was a huge difference between Riley and Tammy. Tammy was always talking about who she had met or who hadn't been at an "in" party. The walk was peaceful until he saw the Land Rover in front of the hotel.

"Oh, no! Do you think it's your family? I'm not ready—"

"Calm yourself, it's Marjorie's car. When my family gets here, it will be en masse via a limo," Conner said.

"You do know that some of them were threatening to come by themselves because they didn't want to bother you," Riley said.

"I know, but they won't. My sisters are just threatening me to see how important me getting my way is," Conner said.

They both went into the inn and dropped their jackets on the sofa.

"Maybe we should—" Riley began.

"It's just us. Let's see what Marjorie wants first," Conner said as he herded Riley into the kitchen.

Sitting in the kitchen eating apple pie was the doctor and Marjorie. Rose was chatting away as they ate.

"Doc, Marjorie," he said in greeting. Both turned to him, and if looks could kill, he would have been in trouble. Conner wasn't used to being in trouble and not knowing the reason. "Is there something we can do for you?"

"Hello," Riley said. "I wanted to thank you both."

"Well, dear, that is why we are here, to check up on you and make sure all is well," Marjorie said, her eyes looking at Conner and then back at Riley. Again, Conner could see that he was the outcast in the room, and he had no idea why.

Marjorie turned towards him and spoke.

"The doctor wanted to check on Riley, and I offered to drive her here. It's good to see that you're doing something with the inn besides just letting it be," Marjorie said. Conner heard the accusation in the tone, but he wasn't getting the problem. This was why he liked numbers. He knew what the problems were, and the problems were clear. He bet Marjorie thought she was telling him exactly what was wrong, and he just couldn't get it.

"Doc, I'm so sorry you came all this way to see me. I'm fine and mobile. I've started reducing the number of pills I'm taking, so I should be good until the end of the week.

The doctor looked at Marjorie and then back at Riley.

"Riley, I wanted to know if I could do an exam on you to close out my hospital records?"

He saw Riley hesitate. If she had protested, he would have told the doctor and Marjorie to leave. However, Riley smiled and then took her to her bedroom. Then Rose left for an errand. He knew what a setup looked like, and he just wanted to know what Marjorie's end goal was.

"So it looks like you've gone through a lot to talk to me. I guess it's a good thing because I'd like to talk to you as well."

Marjorie looked taken back.

"It seems like I'm on your list of people to dislike. I usually know why I'm on that list, and this one just escapes me. Could you give me a heads up on what I've done exactly?"

Marjorie straightened her back and looked him straight in the eye. "There were some questions on how you came about the land you've bought."

"It's not a mystery. I had money, someone needed to sell, and I bought it."

"That seems very cut and dry, but the whole town knows no one would buy up the properties around the inn as long as the Hudson kept the middle property. No one wanted to build around it. It was the thing that held that property in stasis, so to speak, so some new developer wouldn't come to our spot with ideas of making the place by the bay so expensive the inhabitants couldn't live here. We all thought the only reason he would sell is—"

"Is if there was some sort of foul play," Conner finished for her.

"But if you're saying you got the land fair and square,

that means that man is the betrayer to us all," Marjorie whispered. Conner could see her reforming her opinion and finding a new target. He didn't want to be the target, but Hudson was a good guy and didn't deserve her animosity either.

"Don't judge him too harshly. He had some big decisions to make, and I think he did the best he could."

Marjorie held up her hand. "I appreciate you leveling with me, but I think we should just agree to disagree. Since you've been so forthright with me, I'd like to return the favor. I think I need to inquire on how you are doing, Mr. Sanders."

Conner was glad she didn't want to talk about Hudson. It was his story to tell, and he hoped the town gave him a chance to do so.

"I'm listening," Conner said.

"I received a call from a lawyer asking me questions about you and the inn. He claimed that he wanted to know the value of the inn and what it brought in. That he could make it worth my while. He also cautioned me not to get too close to you, Mr. Sanders. He said you would be coming into some bad publicity."

Conner nodded, and in that moment, it all made sense.

"Thank you so much for that bit of information," he said.

"Is there something we can do for you in town, Mr. Sanders?"

He ran through a bunch of scenarios, all of them ending in Marjorie finding out anyway.

"There's nothing you can do. I am dealing with a personal issue at the moment. I'd ask as much as possible if you could keep this to yourself until I finish addressing it, I'd appreciate it."

Marjorie nodded. "You'll find that we protect our own. And whether or not you meant it, you are now a part of the Inheritance Bay family."

Conner laughed. "You know Marjorie; I don't know if I can take being part of another family. I've recently found the pressure of it to be time-consuming."

Marjorie nodded in agreement and then took a breath before she plunged on.

"You leveled with me, and I thought I could do no less. In that same vein, I would ask you to think about doing something in our town. I started the invite program to get some old blood in here again. I knew a lot of them would be older, but there was a hope that maybe they would bring some life back to the town. I want the town I grew up in, not a new resort."

Conner looked at Marjorie and gave her a long look.

"Are you opposed to resorts and progress?"

Marjorie smiled. "No, Mr. Sanders, I'm not opposed to progress, but I think there is something to be said about the heart of the town. That is what I want to make sure is preserved, Mr. Sanders."

Conner looked at Marjorie and could see the empathy and caring in her face. He was conflicted on so many levels now. First, he needed to do something for his parents to show them how much he loved them. It was later he realized how crazy that was, as they all knew he loved them. He had met a friend in this town and tried to help Hudson. Now Marjorie wanted him to help her bring a town back. This wasn't what he signed up for. This was what happened when you were moved by emotional urges and not plans.

He didn't want her hopes to get up. He didn't want her to think he was some hero to come save the day. These days he just wanted to make sure he could quantify his own actions. Just when he was about to try to explain that to her, Riley and the doctor came back.

Riley was all smiles. "I told you so. That should tell you all that you need to know," Riley said. When he looked to the doctor for confirmation, the doctor nodded. Conner looked at Riley.

"Well, then today's trip to Samson and Sugar were gifts that everyone can appreciate, and we can go again now that you've been cleared."

Marjorie cleared her throat. "We'll be going now. We wanted to do the rounds on Riley. Thank you for the ear," Marjorie said. As if by some bell no one could hear, Rose came from downstairs with a pie container.

"Ladies, here's a pie that I had cooling in the downstairs kitchen." The doctor grabbed the container and kissed it.

"Thank you so much. Marjorie is a benevolent cook, but your pie is legendary in town. The couples who stay here rave about it all the time."

"It's my pleasure," Rose replied, blushing as she handed the container over. The doctor looked up at Riley with a wide smile and open gaze.

"Oh, since you are doing better, let me tell you about the Swan Festival. You and Mr. Sanders should come."

"The Swan festival?" Riley asked.

"Yes, it's in a couple of days," the doctor said. "It's a great excuse to get together. It's a highlight of the town, and since you are staying, you want to learn the local customs, right?"

"I do," Riley said hesitantly.

"Okay, so what happens is there is an animal rescue called the Swan's Cove. It takes in all types of animals like beavers, otters, and swans. Then three times a year, we have a festival to release the ones that are ready, if there are any ready to go. So we wait until the veterinarians let us know, and then we start planning the festival.

We've got some birds ready to leave, so vendors are coming: funnel cake, festival food, and games. All of the proceeds go to the Swan Cove."

"It's not chilly to do it now?" Riley asked.

"Chilly for us is just right for some birds. Some stay here, and some fly away. The festival will be amazing. You should come."

Conner saw her indecision and decided to help her out. "I think we can make time for it. It's before Valentine's Day, so it will be great to get out and walk somewhere else besides around the building. Can Merlin come?"

Marjorie looked at the sleeping dog and smiled.

"Yes, as long as he is on a leash, we allow pets. I think it's time we left," Marjorie said.

"Since you've given me a clean bill of health, the least I can do is walk you out," Riley said.

As the women walked through the inn, they took a longer look and commented on the photos and décor. Conner watched them go. He could see Riley standing a little straighter as they pointed to pictures and made comments. When the door was closed, Riley had a radiant smile on her face.

Ten

The day had been electric. She was lying in the most comfortable bed she had ever been in, alone. Merlin was on the floor snoring, but she still couldn't go to sleep. Normally her restlessness could be understood, but tonight, there was something that wouldn't let her settle down. It was that odd time of night. When it was early morning but also kind of late evening, and if a person didn't go to bed soon, it wouldn't be worth it.

She wanted to go over her day. Maybe if she did, she'd be able to put to rest what was riding her.

She had been given a clean bill of health. She knew that, but it was good to hear the doctor confirm it. Her job required her to meet majestic creatures like Samson and Sugar. When she thought about them now, she laughed. They were amazing, and she had expected at any time for them to take a nip out of her, but they hadn't. Conner had said they would go back out to the horses when time permitted.

Conner. She supposed that was the reason she was

running in overdrive. Her initial impression of him had changed from a nonchalant guy with an expensive car to a caring man who liked nice things. She sat up in her bed and looked at Merlin, who was still asleep on the floor. This was the first time they were both secure and happy, and she couldn't go to sleep.

Maybe it was time to take one more look around the inn. She got out of bed and started to wander. She had already found a place for each member of his family. It wasn't easy, but she had picked out each room and then put in a Valentine's Day scrapbook of all of the pictures that were around the inn. Each one had their face on it so she'd know which was which. Again, Rose had been amazing in helping.

The inn was just a canvas that had been painted poorly with cheap ideas. She had walked room to room and scraped off the cheap Hollywood visions and put up visions of love and devotion. Where some rooms were decorated in red velvet, she had the four-poster beds draped in white drapes and the room highlighted with soft pinks and white doves of peace. Where it was dark, she lightened it up, leaving the dark as an accent piece only.

Riley still had some work to be done before she was happy, but her vision was coming true, and it was the most rewarding thing she had done in a long time. Now the only thing she needed to do was stop roaming the inn and find herself back in her really comfy bed so she could get some rest to execute her dreams of grandeur.

She made it back to her bed, and Merlin didn't even flinch when she got in the bed and pulled up the covers. All of her little aches were gone, so there was no excuse why she couldn't get relaxed. Maybe her body needed to be relaxed. Rose had shown her some chamomile tea in the kitchen. She'd make some and be on her way. That's what she needed, a natural relaxer to ease her to sleep.

She walked into the kitchen and looked for a teapot. Then she remembered the electric kettle. She could turn it on, and her water would be done lickety-split. She set it up, turned on the power, and waited. It wasn't even a minute when she saw Merlin.

"Oh, so now you show up? I hope you know I'm not here to get you treats," she said firmly. Riley knew that was a bluff. If he looked at her with those gorgeous eyes and laid down on the ground, she'd bend. Instead of him going into the begging position, she saw his ears perk up, and then he turned and walked down the hall.

Where was he going?

"Merlin?" she whispered. He didn't stop, but as they continued down the hall, she knew where they were going. There were no rooms back here, only offices. Conner's office.

She watched Merlin go into an office, and she knew that Conner must be up as well. There was no time to go back and put on some mature pajamas. She had on her pink-striped pajamas, and that was it. At least she had on the pair with pants and a button top. She knew what she would do. She was going to walk into the office and get her dog.

What was he doing up at this time of night?

She walked into the room and saw him staring at a screen. He hadn't gone to sleep in front of it. He was just staring at it.

"Hey, night owl, what are you doing up?" she asked.

Conner looked away from the screen and looked at her. What she saw on his face was utmost despair. She couldn't leave him here alone.

"Looking for answers in the light?" he replied.

"Wow, if you are looking there, then we've got some real problems. I mean, you're a genius. When the genius guy looks at a blank screen, and that is his best hope, we've all probably got big problems."

"Well, that is one way to look at it," he said.

"Is everything okay?" she asked.

"Yes, it's fine," he said in a small voice.

"Wow, that was the worst lie in history. Why don't you try again or, at the very least, come up with something that sounds better than that? They say the more intelligent you think the person is, the more grandiose the lie," Riley said.

"Is that what they say?" Conner said with a grin. "Then I guess you'll have to come back because I think you deserve something that will take time for me to fabricate," he said.

She walked into the room and took a seat in the chair across from him. "Let this be a lesson that you need to plan ahead. So are you ready to tell me what the problem is?"

"You're so sure you want me to tell you the problem?"

She could see the dark half-moons beneath his eyes. He was exhausted. He had on a dress shirt with sleeves rolled up to his elbows. Whatever it was, he had been at it for a while.

"Yes, I want to hear the problem. Maybe you're too smart, and you need a common view on the situation."

"A common view? You are a lot of things, Riley, but common isn't one of them."

"Enough with the flattery, which I might add is getting you all sorts of brownie points and making you a nicer person by the second," she quipped, hoping to rouse him out of the depressive state he was in.

"I take it you really aren't going to leave."

"You would take that correctly. Now come, come. Confess."

"You first," he said.

Riley was confused, but she shook her head in agreement.

"Are you really feeling better? Or did you just say what the doctor wanted to hear?"

"One, you are very suspicious, and two, I'm fine. It's true I have some aches that come out of nowhere sometimes, but they don't bring me to my knees like they did a couple of days ago. Now it's your turn."

Riley waited for him to speak. The silence stretched between them, and she thought she was going to have to encourage him a little more. Maybe she should just leave him alone. He was a really rich person. In the end, what could she help him with that he couldn't buy?

Then just as she was about to speak, he let out a sigh.

"Well, the truth of the matter is that not so long ago, I thought I wanted to get married to a woman. It was going to be the icing on the cake for my parents for their anniversary. Unfortunately, she decided it was much better business to back out of the arrangement and then sue me for money for her time with me. She wasn't impressed with the Turtle Dove Inn. She thought it was a phase I was going through, but when she realized that I live like this most of the time, she knew we were not compatible, and she needed to be compensated."

Riley didn't move. She couldn't possibly have heard him correctly.

"You are in here over a woman? If she wants to charge you, maybe I need to see what she looks like?"

Conner gave what sounded like a chuckle and then looked at Riley. "It sounds so cliché on both accounts."

She gave him a look over and then tried to clear her mind. "Okay, so just to make sure we are saying the same thing. You two get together. She discovers you like the country, not the city, and now she wants cash? What's the problem? Tell her no?"

"That was my first thought. She's not the first one to try this."

Riley looked at him oddly. She wasn't the first? Wow, she couldn't imagine finding someone and thinking they were the one, but then they just wanted money. That would be bad once, but more than once? She wasn't sure how Conner was able to trust at all. Then a small voice in the back of her head told her it was because whether he wanted to believe it or not, Conner Sanders was a romantic.

"Okay, she's not the first, so what's the problem?"

"She wants me to give her a lot of money; otherwise, she will go to the press and tell them how all of my family was in on it and knew I needed to buy a wife, and she had escaped from my cold clutches."

Then it became clear. While Conner may have had this problem before, it was probably the first time he had to deal with someone who was bringing his family into it.

"Has your family met her?"

"No."

"No? How do you hide the woman who you think you want to marry from your family?"

"It didn't feel right."

"It didn't feel right," she parroted. "I have to tell you that sounds a bit thin."

"I don't know what else to say. I built all of Wealth Builders on my gut, and my gut said no, so I listened. Now she's used that to say I was leading her on."

Riley raised her eyebrows. "Wow, problems of the rich and famous. You got me with this one. I guess my advice would be to stick it out."

"The problem is I came to that conclusion too. I have to say, though, I am tempted to pay her off until after my parents' anniversary," Conner said.

Riley shook her head. "Start as you mean to go."

"You're right."

She gave an exaggerated sigh. "Well, I'll leave you alone since you seem to have the situation well in hand."

"Don't go."

His words were like a balm to her soul. Riley was in such an odd space. She liked a man who was in trouble with another woman threatening him. She turned to him to tell him she had to get some sleep, and again, the despair was a blanket on his features.

Riley couldn't leave him alone like this. She knew this was crazy, but she settled back into the chair.

"I can stay for a few. I mean, maybe I'll get sleepy being in this comfy chair. I want to make sure I finish my vision for each room."

"I think I can get you some latitude with the boss," he said.

"Latitude. You don't know him. I hear he's a workaholic and a perfectionist. I don't know if he knows what latitude is," she joked. When she heard him laugh, the tension drained out of her body, and she let the moment of silence slow between them.

"So the big gathering at Turtle Dove Inn was going to be your way of introducing her?"

He nodded.

She could see how this must have been a huge issue for Conner. He was the one who planned everything, and here he was in a situation that he thought he had under control, but it turned out that he didn't after all. Riley felt bad for the man who had built an empire of security based on his planning and gut instincts. Now they had led him astray, and he was lost. It must have made him question everything he thought he knew about himself.

"Now my life is about making sure the media doesn't find out about my ex."

Riley looked away and said nothing.

"Riley, that was the part when you say, of course, you'll never tell," Conner said.

"It's not my place to say anything, Conner."

Conner cleared his throat and then went on. "Also, I want to make sure my family doesn't know anything either."

Riley gave him a long look before choosing her words carefully. "You think your family is going to be here with you and not know something is off?" she asked.

"They can suspect a lot of things, but it's not the same as if they know."

"Okay, I just don't get it. I can see from the way you are invested in getting everything together for your parents that you love them. This would be one of those times when they would all gather around you, and you'd find that this isn't as big a deal as you thought."

Conner ran his hands through his hair. "That's the problem. I don't want them to deal with my problem. My mom would be indignant. My sisters would want to gather a posse to hunt for Tammy. My dad and brother would be the only sane people, and even then, they would think they had to come to my rescue. I don't need to be rescued and coddled. By not telling them, I can handle it on my own."

"I hear you, but I think the rules changed when she changed them. When she decided to use your family as leverage, it became not just a *you* fight but a family fight."

He rested his head on the headrest and closed his eyes.

"It's my problem first, and that is what I decided. Rose knows, as well as James. I thought they needed to know to fend off potential lawyers or media if it came to that.

Riley heard him but still, the idea of him blocking out so many people who loved him seemed wrong. She took a mental step back and let out a breath. This was his business. She was just the paid help.

"I can tell from your silence that you don't think I'm making the right decision," he said through clenched teeth. "If you keeping silent is going to be a problem, we should address it right here and now."

Riley's eyes popped open, and she waited for him to look at her at least. She waited for nothing.

"You should at least look a person in the eye when you

are threatening their job just to keep your secrets," she said.

He looked tortured but didn't look at her.

"I don't want it to come to that. Just give me some time, Riley. I can figure this out," he said desperately.

Riley was torn, but she was going to put her faith in Conner. She didn't know how but she was sure he would do the right thing. He did the right thing by her, and he would have done the right thing by Merlin.

"You're in luck. I allow one deep dark secret per inn. Consider your dark secret token used."

"Thank you, Riley."

"Don't thank me yet. I want you to answer a question," Riley asked.

"Go for it."

"Why are you letting me meet your family?"

Eleven

Riley didn't expect him to answer.

"My gut says yes," he answered.

So on the one hand she had the approval of his gut. Riley laughed to herself. Every woman wanted to be able to say, "Yeah, he knew I was the one when his greater intestines approved me."

"So tell me, why hotel management?" he asked.

Riley was actually grateful for the topic switch.

"My story is pretty simple. I like to make homes," she said. "I started out as a waitress who liked to decorate her station. Then I graduated to a cook who plated well. It was good to be able to make a home in any place. One that people wanted to come back to.

"I don't have a lot of memories of my mom. I know that when I reached my teens my dad was a different person and it was, at best, strained between us. He was stuck with a kid who reminded him of his one true love. He took jobs that required him to travel, and I just got better at making homes of places and things. I had this hope that one day he'd want to stay in a home that I had built, but it wasn't to be."

"From looking around the inn and hearing your story, you must be pretty good at making homes; otherwise, no one would call you back."

"I like to think so."

"The places that got you were lucky. You brought a piece of you and shared it with so many people," he said.

She let his words settle into her. Conner hadn't known how many years she thought she was making a home, and then her father wouldn't show.

"Sorry, didn't mean to bring my dirty laundry to light—"

"It's no problem. Riley, I am interested in everything about you."

Okay, that was her cue. She had stayed and been the shoulder to confess on, but now it was time to go. They were firmly crossing the employer/employee line. They both stood up at the same time.

"I think it's time for me to go to bed." Conner smiled. "I was thinking… I'm glad we met. True, not in the best of circumstances, but I think it was the best, like we were destined."

"It's funny to me that Mr. Facts-and-Figures believes in destiny."

He took another step towards her. "Using a little bit of your intuition, anyone would be able to do what I do," he said.

The timbre of his voice seeped into her, causing a shiver of recognition. He was looking into her eyes as if he saw something there that he would never let out of his sight. His gaze was so intense that she wasn't sure how she stood underneath it.

Her breath quickened, but it was only after hearing the telltale catch that she knew she wasn't as immune as she would have liked to believe. Riley was reciting in her head all of the reasons that she and Conner wouldn't work. The longer she stood in front of Conner, the more intent he seemed. Maybe it was a syndrome that because she had listened to him, he was uber grateful and interested in her? She didn't think so because if there was such a syndrome, so many people would be making poor decisions about their love lives in greater numbers.

"Umm, I think that this may be our cue to go to bed. Uh, I mean for me to go back to my bed, by myself. Wow, I'm really stumbling over myself," Riley said.

It was unfortunate that she hadn't practiced any special hand signals with Merlin for occasions like these. How could this even happen? He had clearly just been scammed by a woman; this was probably just a rebound moment. She had forgotten about the rebound. Now it was starting to make sense to her. He had told her his story, and she had fallen for it. He had found a person who would listen, and it was such a big difference from the woman scamming him that he thought he had feelings. There was the explanation for the impossible situation she found herself in right now.

Riley was a practical woman, after all. It might start out okay, but as time went on, their differences would tear them apart, and she'd end up in a town where seeing the man was a problem. Then she'd have to leave again.

"Am I keeping you, Riley?"

"Yes—No... What I mean is that I've enjoyed our time."

Wow, was it silent in the night? The glow from the computer screens cast him in an eerie light that made him look almost ethereal. She needed to move now. No one was talking, and it was clear that she should be moving on now.

"Get some rest," she said, hoping the phrase would help her body to move out of its perpetual state of stillness.

"I will as soon as I do this," he said. Then the world started to tilt as she heard her name whispered from his lips. Next, the shadow of his head covered her as his head bent down and lowered his mouth to hers.

Was this really happening?

Riley stood there and let the moment engulf her. Conner had brought one hand to her chin to hold her in place while he delivered a dream. Riley could officially say it was true that dream kissers had fresh breath and smooth lips. No dry scratching was going on here. His kiss was everything that she had dreamed about but had called herself foolish for wanting. There was a little voice that asked her why she would want to start something she couldn't finish. Riley promptly ignored that voice and told it to feel his warm lips and the delicate way those lips went over hers.

The thing that had been flitting between them had come out to be seen in a big way. It was a classic story of following how you felt. This attraction broke down barriers between them and cleared a path for something more.

He might have taken the finance world by storm, but

this kiss was all about asking and permissions. The kiss was questing and sweet. It was the way he asked when he could have easily taken that made him so irresistible.

Riley would have been able to snap out of it had he stormed the castle, but he asked for permission, and she gave it. There was something so moving to her when a person could take or dictate, but they tempered themselves and let another person choose. It made her feel safe. It made her feel like this man would always respect her and never take advantage of her.

For so long, it had been just her and Merlin. And before Merlin, she had been alone. When she leaned into the kiss, his hand went from her chin and traced the side of her jaw until he had traced her ear, sending tremors through her body until his hands threaded into her hair and brought her closer.

She could have stayed there forever in his embrace. She might have given it a try if it weren't for Merlin's low whine that ruined the moment as surely as if a parent had walked into the room.

Her eyes popped open, and then she looked at the man she was kissing and pulled back. After many hours of sensible talk, she had thrown it all away when Conner kissed her. She wouldn't regret it, though, because it was a once in a lifetime experience, but now that she had tested the waters, it was time to come back to reality. She stepped back and tried to control her breathing so he wouldn't know how much the kiss affected her.

"Riley," he murmured.

She looked up at him and waited. She knew kissing him again was a huge mistake and would solidify a sneaky suspicion she had about how she felt about him. However, she felt powerless to stop him if he asked. Instead of saying anything, he looked at her and smiled.

"I want you to know I don't normally kiss my employees," he said with a hint of uncertainty in his voice. All at once, her apprehension melted away to hear he wasn't as unaffected as he looked.

She gave him a small smile and let out a sigh.

"I'm not human resources, but it's a good thing you've got this kissing thing controlled. Think about all the work you'd miss out on if you had to kiss every employee in Wealth Builders."

Conner laughed, and there was relief in his voice as if he weren't sure what to expect, but that she was unexpected and nice all at the same time.

"I meant to say that because you are working here, this thing that happened between us is between us as adults, not as employee and employer. It was a lapse on my part, and I'm sorry. It's not my intention to put you in an awkward position."

Riley knew her smile was in place. She had practiced for too long, keeping it in place, not to know how it felt when it was in place. He had just taken one of the most magical moments she had ever had and reduced it to a lapse in judgment.

"I understand. I do think it's really late now. If you'll excuse me."

"Of course."

Riley walked to her room by memory. She didn't run, and she didn't see any of the work that she had worked so hard on. When she got closer to the kitchen, she smelled the heat from the water. The kettle would keep it warm and turn off by itself, but she was the help, and she should remember to follow the rules. So she went into the kitchen and unplugged the kettle, and then went to her room.

When she got to her room, she closed the door and then sat up in the bed. What had happened? She was pulling in deep breaths to keep the heat from spilling from her eyes.

It was a kiss that shouldn't have been. It was a kiss that she had been waiting for. It was all of those things all at the same time.

She put her hand to her cheek and could still feel the warmth of him on her there. He had a unique smell that was probably his soap, but it lingered. Like the kiss, his scent was fading, and with it, her foolish fog of loneliness. That was the only thing that she could attribute this to.

Riley worked around men all the time in the kitchen and in the hotel, and not once had she ever looked at them as men. They were just bodies to help her accomplish a task. Getting entangled on the job had been the thing to avoid at all cost. When her boss had taken an interest in her, she had been surprised and dismayed.

If she were honest, she could have seen her feelings coming a mile away. When was the last time she had someone she could depend on? Conner didn't realize how his easy nature and answer for everything reeled people in to feel safe and secure. She supposed her mother had been nurturing, but when she passed, her father had set her on a lonely road. She hadn't ever found a person who took the time to know her, and it figured the one time she thought she had found such a person, he'd be rich and totally out of her league.

She lay down and closed her eyes. She knew the answer. Loneliness had snuck up on her and gotten under her defenses. She laid down and tried to reset her barriers. She knew how to keep others out and to keep safe. Riley thought about Conner's statement that he didn't haggle. That man was haggling all the time; he just didn't know it. He just didn't know he had the goods that everyone wanted.

Normally he found answers in his numbers, but there were no numbers for the kiss he had just shared with Riley. What had he been thinking? How did he think that was going to end? Conner tried to find different reasons that the kiss happened Maybe it was the confession, or maybe it was the night, or maybe he just had no clue.

Maybe it was time that he was honest with himself. The truth was that the feelings he felt for Riley had been building since he met her. If he looked at the trend of things, this was the only end that made sense.

In the midst of trying to get rid of Tammy and her poison, he had found the woman he had always wanted. She was kind, considerate, and so giving that she left nothing for herself. She had brown eyes that were so expressive and an energy that never seemed to waiver.

She called to him on every level. Her wit was refreshing. She was shy in some moments and on a crusade for things she cared about. He hadn't thought he would find any woman attractive after the burn of Tammy. He hadn't told

Riley all of it, but Tammy wasn't the first to try and get money from him. She was just the smartest and had bided her time to find out what was really important to him.

So now that he had faced that Riley was the woman for him and had all the characteristics he thought he'd never find, he had one more thing to address. How would he do anything if she worked for him? Employee loyalty was one thing, but office romances were not encouraged. Heck, he was having problems with a regular romance, much less an office one.

The factors in this deal were getting more and more complicated. There was also one other consideration that he had to factor in. Maybe she didn't want to do anything forever. Riley had just moved to town. She was here to get her bearings and set up her new life. She thought he was just passing through. Maybe she didn't want to hitch herself to a man in the middle of a lawsuit. No problem, Conner had a plan. He would keep himself distant from her. He would address the Tammy issue and, when he was free, see if all was well.

He gave himself a nod for a good solution reached. The solution was so easy he wondered why he had fretted about it. This is one of those times that him finding a solution would be appreciated in the end. In the end, Riley would thank him for this plan.

Conner, on the other hand, would have to find a way to see Riley every day and not reminisce about that kiss. She had teased him and said he was the one that haggled, but it wasn't true. She was the one who was haggling. There was no sense in haggling with Riley; she was the one who was the prize.

Twelve

"Rose, I'm going into town to take a look at things," Riley said. "I've been there, but most of my time has been at the inn. Today is a slow day, and I don't expect any more deliveries, so I'll be going into town. Did you want anything?"

"No, dear, go along. Are you taking Merlin?"

Rose tried to sound nonchalant, but Riley knew she had formed such an attachment to Merlin that she had to wonder if she had lost her dog.

"No, I'm going to be going store to store, and he hasn't been back in town since the accident. I wouldn't want to take him on such a long trip, that is, if you don't mind?"

Rose smiled down at Merlin, patting his head. Her adoration was clear in her gaze, and Merlin's feelings were clear as well as he lay on the ground and exposed his belly for rubbing.

"Make sure you get back in time. You know Conner is coming back today. I told him two days is more than enough time in the city."

Riley nodded and then went out to the car. As she waited for it to heat up, she tried not to let her thoughts drift back to a kiss that had heated her up just fine. She wasn't a child. This wasn't her first kiss, but it was definitely her more memorable one. In truth, Riley had to wizen up. Conner's thoughts on their kiss had been clear when he avoided her like the plague the day after. Where before he had checked in with her every day, he hadn't even bothered to come down when she was at breakfast. That evening when dinner was served and Riley asked if she should get another plate, Rose mentioned that Conner had left and would be back in a couple of days.

It took all of Riley's discipline to sit through that meal and smile. All the while inside, she thought she had just driven him away from his own home. Yes, it was clear what he thought about their kiss. Riley knew she should be grateful to Conner. He understood that it was impossible and had put some distance between them.

Riley had to admit that she had been very productive these last two days. With him gone, she could work from sunup to sundown. When Rose and James went to bed, she could walk the inn and see what her vision looked like in the daylight and at night.

Rose stuck her head out the door and saw her sitting in her car. Riley hoped she didn't ask her what she was thinking because she wasn't sure she could even come up with something that made sense.

"By the way, Riley, there's an antique shop in town if you want to look at it. I heard you talking to the contractor about having some heritage pieces, and you might find some there," Rose said.

Riley nodded as the car warmed up. She had a place she could start. She had to make her own connections in town if this was going to work. Looking online and in books worked sometimes, but there was nothing like picking the pieces out of a store.

She was proud of the way she had tastefully transformed the inn. She hadn't shown Conner yet, but even the brochures had been updated. James had been the helping hand to say the look shouldn't go to waste.

Riley may not ever be considered chic for a hotel decorator, but she knew how to make a place cozy. The inn was small enough to feel like just a large home and big enough to have different tones in it. She planned on living here, and she'd be able to look at the Turtle Dove Inn and know that she had done that. She wanted to get the little touches she had put all around the inn approved by Conner, but he had left. If he didn't like what she had done, it would be his fault. Fortunately, she had Rose go over the designs and cosign on it all.

She hoped that the kiss hadn't changed everything. She wanted to make the inn a memorable experience for his family. Riley hoped that the kiss wouldn't make him want to throw out everything she had done. She shook her head and found herself at the same light where she had met Conner. When the light turned green, she noticed the road had been fixed. Well, that was something. In small towns, it seemed like things got done.

Riley thought about the motel she had passed to get to this spot. In more ways than one, she was so grateful that Larry had sent her away. Riley also wanted to talk to Marjorie. Riley's agreement was to work with Larry. She wanted to make sure she could still stay in Inheritance Bay even though she wasn't with Larry. More importantly, the letter had said that after the apprenticeship, she would get her own home and land. Was that still true?

She was sure she'd work it out. It didn't take long to find the antique store. There were a lot of stores that seemed like they were empty. The antique store she headed toward was called Gentle Memories. When she stepped through the door, the bell rang, and she was wrapped up in the smell of vanilla and what smelled like cake batter. It was a haven. Each item was laid out in a semi scene with handwritten yellow tags on each thing. Riley was in heaven.

She saw heart-shaped items all around and headed to the items that were in sets.

"Hello?" Riley called out.

"Are you lost? I'm coming?" a voice called out.

Riley laughed.

"I'm not lost. I want to buy some items."

Marjorie came from the back. "Oh, Riley, it's you. I didn't expect to see you, but I'm glad you are here. Welcome to Gentle Memories."

"Thank you, I love the way you've laid out everything."

"Oh, I'm glad. I change it up for holidays and seasons. This month the trail through the store is a heart."

Riley looked, and sure enough, it was. "That's brilliant. I wanted to see if there were some items I could get for the inn."

"Of course. Is Merlin outside?"

Riley shook her head. "No, I left him at the inn. I

wasn't sure how long I'd be, and he hasn't been in town since the incident."

"Marjorie, are you coming back?" a voice called from the back.

Marjorie clasped her hands and smiled. "You have perfect timing! Did you eat lunch yet?"

"No, it's a little early for me and—"

"Of course it is. It's a little early for us all, but we need to make it early so we can have our girl talk. By the time we all go round-robin and discuss the issues, we find we barely have enough time to eat lunch. Come along. You're going to be living here, you need to know the girls."

"I do?" Riley said with uncertainty in her voice.

"Of course. I don't know your plans, but at least say hello. We're all a part of the group that made the program to bring people back to Inheritance Bay. We're actually the town council. It's hard to get things done when you're sitting in a stuffy office. Here we can talk freely amongst friends."

Riley nodded her head, not really sure why they thought they couldn't speak anywhere in town. Was there some secret about the real state of affairs in the town? But she nodded anyway and was walked back into a kitchen where a group of women were cooking desserts and laughing. She expected a lot of things, but this wasn't one of them. Marjorie clapped her hands, and all of the chattering stopped, and four pairs of eyes turned to her.

Riley recognized the doctor, who was the first to wave to her. "Riley, you are looking better, so I'm glad you came into town. Did you bring Merlin?"

Knowing at least one person made the odd and uncomfortable situation bearable. "Merlin isn't here. If I know him, he's living it up being waited on hand and foot by Rose at the house."

The doctor nodded and then leaned forward as she asked her question.

"You don't have to answer. In fact, if you told me it was none of my business, I wouldn't be offended, but I have to ask. Marjorie told me that instead of doing your apprenticeship with Larry, you're helping Mr. Sanders out?"

The other women fell silent and turned to face her. "You're staying at Turtle Dove?" a young woman asked, sitting in ripped jeans and a half shirt that said, Dare me!

"Yes, I'm there for now," Riley said, unsure why it was such a big deal one way or another.

"So do you think his looks make up for how heartless he is?" the other woman asked. Riley swung her gaze to the other woman, who was dressed in khakis.

The first woman looked at Riley as she waited for an answer.

"So you're staying at the Turtle Dove Inn? Is he swimming in money like they say?" one of the women asked.

Riley looked at the group and wondered what had happened here to turn the nice group of gossiping women into a pride of lionesses sniffing out a target. They didn't know Conner. Conner flaunting wealth was so not him. She didn't speak but looked at the last woman, who was about Marjorie's age. When she gave Riley a once over, she smiled.

"Does he treat you right at that place?" the older woman asked.

Riley smiled and then nodded. "He does right by me, and looking at how pickings are slim for jobs, I could have done worse."

The other woman agreed and then turned back to the large table they were all sitting at rolling out cookies.

"Okay, ladies, I'm glad you've contained yourselves and your questions. We all know Riley from the accident with Mr. Sanders, but she was one of the first to answer our communications to relocate here."

"You look young. Are you running from something?" the older woman asked. "My life would have to be pretty bad for me to relocate sight unseen."

Riley thought maybe she had counted her luck too early. Was she running from something?

"I wasn't running, but I didn't know what I was going to do either. So this opportunity came at the right time."

The doctor jumped in and sighed. "I'm not sure about the opportunity, but you're right, it's a job. The fact is there could be more jobs if he did something with the buildings he bought."

Marjorie held up her hand and looked around the room. "I think that Mr. Sanders is going to do right by us. He may have to take care of other matters as well before he can focus on the area."

Riley looked at Marjorie and wondered if Conner had told her about his ex.

The doctor got up and wiped her hands on her apron. "Well, while he tries to find the meaning of life and entertain his family, he has made Inheritance Bay a ghost town for his personal pleasure. If he doesn't say what he is going to do with this property, then no one wants to move next to abandoned buildings"

Marjorie took Riley to the sidebar where there were small sandwiches. She leaned her head closer to Riley as if they were co-conspirators.

"Please excuse the group. We have all been here in the bay for a while. When you've seen it at its peak, it can hurt to see it this way. The streets are empty, and here we are preparing for the Swan Festival, and the normal environmentalist and nature lovers aren't lining our streets yet. They might come in on the day of the festival, but they used to come for the week."

Riley looked back at the women talking around the large table. "Surely Conner can't be responsible for everything that everyone is talking about. I mean, I've seen what he bought."

"Conner bought the land adjacent to his property as well as every other third property in the Bay within twenty miles of the inn. We have ordinances. If you want to build and you have a neighbor, you have to get approval from him as the closest landowner, Marjorie said"

"Isn't that a bit odd?" Riley asked.

Marjorie shook her head.

"The people who built this town were more friends than businessmen. They didn't want to offend, so we have very friendly by-laws. We could go to court and get the bylaw removed, but the bylaws are the only thing that has stopped developers from coming. We have been to court twice this year, and those bylaws have helped our position to preserve our town. Twice, and its only February."

"How does Conner play into this?" Riley asked.

"He's not here enough to be called on for meetings. He doesn't take schedules on a timely basis. Anyone who buys realizes they will have to deal with him, or at the very least, work with him. Saying you need to see or deal with Conner Sanders is like dealing with the boogeyman. He personally handles the deals in town, so he intimidates most people away. Between his reputation and booked schedule, it's almost impossible to get him to a table to negotiate or ask anything."

Riley heard what Marjorie was saying, but the cold, calculated man they had built in their minds wasn't the man that had kissed her so passionately a couple of nights ago. They didn't know him, and Conner was otherwise engaged and unable to see what was going on right in front of him.

Thankfully, when she returned to the table, the conversation had turned to the proper way to roll out cookie dough and who was going to have problems when their cookies came out. When they had placed the last tray in the oven and trays of piping hot cookies were coming out, she stood up.

"Thank you, ladies, but I've got to finish my work and get back to my Merlin," she said to Marjorie. "I saw a yellow post-it pad out there. How about the items that I'd like I put a post-it note on it? Are you okay with that?"

"Of course. Just make sure you put quantities on it if you see something you want more than one of. Sometimes we get items in by the dozen."

Riley looked around the store and had to control herself. She was sure she could find a use and a season for most of the items in the store. Picking just for Valentine's was a chore. When she was done, Marjorie was at the register.

"I'm so sorry, I didn't mean to interrupt—"

"No, dear, it's fine. I'm glad you came. I think the others needed to see that you can be around Mr. Sanders for a while and not turn into a zombie."

"I'm glad I could help change some hearts and prove he's not a monster. He might be driven but he's not malicious."

"Does Merlin like him?" Marjorie asked.

Riley smiled and nodded.

"Well, then, that's good enough for me. Animals can smell evil," Marjorie said.

Thirteen

Note to self: Be wary of gatherings of women. They could be women gathering to make cookies or gathering to run the town. As Riley slid into her car, she put the key into the ignition when her phone rang. It was Rose, and she immediately thought something was wrong with Merlin.

"Hello, Rose?"

"Oh my goodness, I'm so glad that I caught you. It seems that Conner is on his way home. He's had a long day and an even longer flight. I asked him to pick you up."

"Me? Why? I have James's car with me."

"I know, dear. But he's been traveling for hours. I know he worked on the plane, and he was on a long flight. It makes me nervous for him to come home by himself. Driving alone isn't the best thing for him. I would send a car, but he has so much pride that he's making me gray early."

Riley completely understood. "Okay, tell me what to do with James's car and where to meet Conner."

"Thank you, Riley. James will pick up the car tomorrow. Wait in front of the store where you first met."

Riley murmured under her breath, *how could I forget our fateful meeting?* It took her twenty minutes to find a space for James's car, and by the time she was done, she was just getting to the meet spot when Conner rolled up in his car.

"Great! I'm glad you're here. I didn't want you to wait," Conner said.

She got into the car and was surrounded by the smell of Conner. Riley had to mentally tell herself not to moan. It had only been a few days, and his scent was enough to take her back to the kiss. She needed to pull it together. Riley looked at him as he pulled the car away from the curb. He was tired, and his hair looked as if he had run his hands through it several times, leaving trenches. His hands held on to the wheel, and every so often, she would see his hands flex.

When the car stopped at a light, she thought she saw him close his eyes and take in a deep breath. When he turned to look at her, there was raw want and need in his eyes. She had no words for the way his look pinned her in place. The light turned, and like clockwork, he turned to the light and then moved the car along.

Now being in the enclosed space was just proving that she needed to work on blocking him out. Instead of reminiscing over a kiss that couldn't lead anywhere, she needed to think about what she and Merlin would do when this was over? She wasn't really working with Larry, so what would the town let her do? There were more questions and not enough answers. But she knew she would come up with something. She always did. Just when she thought this ride was going to happen in silence, he decided to break it.

"Hi, Riley, I'm glad I caught you."

"Rose let me know a few minutes ago. If the call had come a little later, we would be racing to see who could get home first," Riley said.

He nodded his head.

"I'm glad I caught you. I heard that there could be some snow today. You're still new here, so I thought I could bring you home."

Home? Did he really mean it as their home?

"Thank you for coming. I hadn't heard about the snow, but I admit I would have been nervous driving alone in the snow."

"There's no need to thank me, Riley. We're still friends, right?" Conner said.

It was odd because right then, Riley didn't know. What she did know was she was confused. Could she be his friend? Being friends would mean they would be around each other during the day, and she wasn't sure she could do that.

"You're my boss first and my friend second. As my boss, of course, I would do what you asked. As my friend, if you wanted to leisurely go through the town picking up all sort of Valentine's Day décor, I would definitely have to go with you—to help you pick out the right items, of course."

He smiled and kept driving. "Well, it's good to know that you won't let something like shopping come between us," he said.

"No, I find shopping to be a bonding experience between friends," Riley said with a smile.

For the next few moments, he drove in silence. The silence helped to settle her nerves and allowed her breathing to come back to normal. This was Conner. He was just a man, a gorgeous man with a kind heart and lots of money, but a man nonetheless.

"How was your trip?" she asked.

"It was what I thought it would be. Same old, same old. How has the inn been? Did you find all that you needed?"

"I've found it, and it's either in the inn or will be here in a day or two. The items that are en route are accent items. The bulk of the work is done."

"Did you sleep while I was gone? It seems like you'd have to be up all night long to get this done."

"I told you, once I see a house and I see the real charm of the it, it becomes easy. When you can't find the thing that makes a place special, then things can go slow."

"Well, then I'm glad you've managed to tap into the heart of the house. We may need it," he murmured.

She wanted to ask him how things had gone with the ex, but under no circumstances did she think that was appropriate.

"You were in town. Did you find any hidden gems there?"

She remembered the cookie session at Marjorie's shop and felt like she had to say something.

"You know, Conner, the people here are looking to you to help them bring the town back to what it was. You bought the surrounding properties because of personal family issues, not wanting any of the properties to be used to spy on what is going on at the inn, but you need to think about what your actions will mean for the town."

"The town? I think the town wants me to leave it as soon as possible," he snorted.

"Conner, do you believe that?" she asked.

Conner let out a breath. "No, I don't. But I don't want to be a savior either. So I'm curious, were you ambushed in town?"

"No, I was shopping in Marjorie's shop, and it turns out the town council gathers there over cookie making. I came in while they were in the middle of rolling dough."

Conner laughed. "That is one of the things I really like about this place; they have their own way of doing things."

Riley smiled. Conner was right. It did seem like there was the Inheritance Bay way, and then there was what others might do. She had to admit she liked the bay way. If only she could find a way to stay in the same town with Conner without making a fool of herself.

He needed to keep his hands on the wheel, so he didn't reach for her. Conner had been tense until Riley had gotten into the car. As soon as he'd gotten in his car at the airport, he called Rose to find Riley. When Rose said she was in town, he knew he couldn't wait until he got to the inn to see Riley.

When she sat in the car, he felt the electricity. Was she

remembering the last time they were alone? Did she remember the kiss? He did. In fact, he hadn't been able to think about much else, much to the chagrin of his lawyers, who kept asking for his input and views on different matters when he was at the home office.

He knew everyone in the company thought he was preoccupied with the situation going on with his family. It was no secret that family was important to him. Conner didn't bother to correct them.

Yes, his mind was preoccupied. It was preoccupied with silky brown hair. It was obsessed with soft, pink lips and skin so smooth that it begged to be touched. Nothing could erase her image from his mind. When the subject of his ex was brought up, he wondered what he had been thinking. Tammy had never wanted the small-town life. She had never wanted to go to the charity balls his family and him held multiple times throughout the year. Still, he knew it wasn't all Tammy's fault. He'd wanted to be with someone and grow with someone, and he'd rushed it. His mother's words came to him.

"Conner, some things can't be rushed or bought. They come when they come. Most of the time when you're not expecting them."

Riley was the proof of that in his life. It was the cadence of her voice he found soothing as he drove. Then he started to listen to what she was saying.

"I think they are trying to find out how you do things as well, Conner. They're doing that by waiting to see what you're going to do for the town," she said.

"You keep saying what I'm going to do for the town. I'm not here for the town. I'm here for my parents."

"I hear you, but this town is trying to build itself up. They've sent out these letters to have people come back and you've taken up a lot of real estate that might lure people to come back here if it were available for rent. Some of your places are good spots for people who want to open businesses, but they can't open one because you own it and you haven't decided what you are going to do with it. And you picked them all up at the same time, giving the town no chance to try to buy it from you."

Conner tried to be objective. The purchasing of the buildings had been a perfect storm. He had come with Tammy. The idea had germinated on what to do for his parents. Tammy had made some off remark saying the only way this town would be fit was if someone bought it and then transformed it into something livable.

In hindsight, he should have gotten the hint then and there that this type of life wasn't for her. Instead, he had looked at the city records online and found a couple of the buildings that were behind on taxes. He made an offer to the owner, and then he found himself with a large enough part of the town that he could rebuild it if he wanted to. At the time, he had thought Tammy would want to do the rebuilding, but when he had suggested it to her, she had laughed at him and told him not to joke in such a manner.

"The intention wasn't as aggressive as you make it seem." Conner knew what a takeover was, and this was nowhere near it. This had just been what happened when a person with money wanted to make a relationship that was going nowhere work.

"No one can say what was going on in your head. What the town can agree on is that the plan they hatched to get people to come back is in danger. They can't tell people the town is in a growth phase when you don't want to do anything with your properties. Turtle Dove Inn is a bit removed from the town. The inn doesn't even tell people to go back to the town and enjoy any of the stores. It basically doesn't do anything for the town."

Conner let out a breath and thought about what Riley was saying. "I think they are really putting too much stock in what I do. From the beginning, I've always said I'm here for my family. I'll do something for the town while I'm here, but I don't think I want to make a commitment."

Riley sighed. "I think that is the concern. You don't want to stay here. The bay will fall off your radar. You'll at best tell someone on your team to fix the income issues which might come with upgrading everything and then leeching away the small-town feel of the town. They don't want to become some resort place."

Conner grunted. "I think the town needs to make up its mind. First, they don't want me here. Now I'm here, they want me to spend money to help it get to a certain place, but they don't want it to go to a place that obviously makes money. Lots of small towns have charm, and they are resort spots," he argued.

He heard her shift in her seat.

"Really, Conner? Do you think that if we had had our accident in a resort community, it would have been settled like this? Do you think the doctor would have come out to the inn? Do you think that Marjorie and the council would be able to hold council meetings while baking cookies?"

"Okay, maybe not, but the fate of the town, which is

resting on my shoulders as you would have me believe, hasn't been the main focus of my life."

"Conner, I understand that you have other issues that are taking precedence, but you can't blame these women for being concerned. They live here, Conner. The stores aren't just businesses they do as a side thing. The businesses are their bread and butter. They look at their businesses, and this is the sum total of what they live for, pass on to their children and socialize around. I know you know the numbers. This town has a plan to pull itself up, but you can see it has some ways to go. They think they can do it, but whether you mean to or not, you are a barrier that they have to address at some point. Unless you give them a plan or some sign of what it is that you are going to do here."

"Why does it matter to you, Riley?" he asked.

He could see her flinch, and then she took a breath. "I came here for a new start. This isn't just some random town we are talking about in a book. We're talking about the place I'm going to call home. I'd like to know it had a chance. You know, one of the things that convinced me to come here was the history of the town. It used to be a bay for smugglers and thieves. The bay was discovered, and a majority of the men were taken from the town. The women had to find a way to protect it.

The first thing they did was make offices. The sheriff's office, the banking office, and the farmer's office. So no one would guess right away that they had a shortage of men, the sheriff's office was named Tom Marshall, Sheriff's Office. They included male names in the titles. It worked while they found mail-order grooms. The women knew how to run the town because the men were away most of the time anyway. As the grooms came and stayed, the town grew back.

"They made sure to keep the arts, crafts, appraisals, and things they did year-round to keep the town alive. About ten to fifteen years ago, people started leaving for the city. When they did, the town tried to be a tourist spot. They showcased the smuggler's port, but there weren't enough people who would stay once business seemed like it was picking up. The young people just wanted to leave and there weren't enough stores that stayed open to keep the tourist coming to the town once again had to be saved by bold out of the box thinking.

They sent the notes out to those who had been here fifteen to twenty years ago and asked them to come back be trained and take a chance. I think a town that can do that to save itself is something I want to be a part of. It's an inheritance that's worth risking it all on."

Conner hadn't known the past. He hadn't taken the time to even find out about what was. Riley had done more than he had before he had bought up the properties. She was right. He hadn't given it any thought, but he could see that hadn't been the right way.

"You're right. I haven't done my due diligence. Let me get past the anniversary, and then I'll sit with Marjorie to come up with a long-term plan, okay?"

"Thank you, Conner. If you and Marjorie come up with a plan, I'm sure she'll be able to get everyone on board. I think you'll find the attitude of the town will change once they find out you want to do something that will help them stabilize the town."

Conner laughed. "You do realize that I've been here significantly longer than you, and you already know the key players, the history, and the path. That's pretty fantastic."

"It's nothing. I think you would know the same thing if you weren't otherwise occupied. You have already met with the women, and I think you'll find they are passionate and fair. When people want to do something to make something work, it will always work better than someone who wants to do something in order to be right."

"It's true."

"Being right or being the ones that come up with all of the ideas is not important to them at all. What is important to them is saving their home, and to that end, you'll find you have a bunch of allies in this town."

"As usual, Riley, you are full of surprises. You seem to really have a talent for reading people."

"It's a skill I needed as a child. When my dad worked all the time, and I stayed with family and friends, I had to get the lay of the land quickly. I think it's always better to think everything over twice and err on the side of caution."

Conner could hear the lessons in her voice. He could imagine it wasn't a skill that she always got right. He had to think how fortunate he was. The Sanders came and picked him up when other families had just left him or brought him back. He didn't have the horror stories that other kids had. Listening to Riley, he didn't even have some of the stories that kids who had birth families had.

"Listen, I'm glad you have the skill. It must serve you well when you are working in the hotel business and dealing with staff. I personally surround myself with people who are understanding that I'm not always in the moment. I can deal with people, but numbers are my preferred companion."

"I think this preference for numbers is due to the bad luck you are having with women."

Conner laughed. Riley would have been the only one to try to make a joke of his bad luck with women. She didn't accuse him of leading women on. In fact, he had to say that she was among the few who didn't look at him and automatically assume that he had used his money to get his way in the relationship.

"I'll admit that situation is not helping my social skills," Conner said.

He drove up to the inn, and then she gave him a look as her hand was on the door.

"Any word on the standoff? The day is almost upon us, and it would be nice if you could enjoy the day with everyone else coming."

Conner couldn't agree with her more. "There's been some posturing but nothing firm. Right now, it's still a game of chicken, but the good thing is no matter which way it goes, it's almost over."

There was something so comforting about being able to confide in another person who wasn't your family. Riley was resilient and beautiful on the inside and the outside. The kiss was just the beginning of what he wanted from her. Distance had given him clarity, and he knew who and what he wanted.

"When something happens, you are going to have to act fast and decisively. Do you really think that on the day when you are all supposed to be together that no one will notice that you are not yourself? Share with them, Conner. Let them be there for you so you aren't bearing this burden alone."

"You don't understand my family," he said. And in a moment, his thoughts went to protecting his family. Who was Riley to tell him what to do with his family? What did she know about them?

"Conner, from everything you've said, it seems like they would want to be with you and band together. You just leaving them out is going to seem odd. You set up all of this for one day, and then you have to leave to address an emergency. It won't add up."

"Who says it won't?"

"Conner, they know you. I can tell when the lawyers call you because you get that far-away look on your face. It's so apparent that something is wrong. Your family will notice."

Conner turned so he was fully facing her.

"You don't know my family. You don't understand," he said as he thought about all the worry he would be causing them for nothing. They couldn't fix it. No one could fix anything until the money request was made. It was all a waiting game. Besides, it could be that nothing happened, and then it would have been for nothing that he had worried them. No, he knew what he was doing.

"Conner, they are your bedrock. It seems odd that you wouldn't share with them this moment. The burden would be lighter if you did."

His phone rang, and he could see it was a lawyer. All of a sudden, this conversation was just one more thing to manage. He was methodical as always. He would take care of Riley first and then call the lawyer back.

"Let us be clear. When my parents come, you will not speak of this. You don't have to agree or understand what I'm doing. Your job is to make sure they have a perfect time, and that is it. It is not in your job description to give me advice on having family, especially as none of it would have come from first-hand experience."

And just like that, the words fell out of his mouth, and he would have given anything to be able to take them back. He heard her gasp, and if it were possible, he felt smaller than a flea. The phone was still ringing, and he took it out of his pocket to let them know he'd call them back. Then he saw Riley exiting the car.

"Ugh! Riley I—"

She held up her hand. "You know what? You're right. I'm going to stay in my lane as the paid staff, and you do you with your family. What does a single child know anyway about how families operate?"

She got out of the car, slammed the door behind her, and went into the inn. A few moments later, a text showed up on his phone from the lawyer.

"No word yet."

Conner watched her go into the inn and just laid his head back on the headrest. He beat his hand against the steering wheel and then laid his head on the wheel. She didn't understand, or maybe he didn't understand. It didn't matter, this situation was out of control. He had no way to make it better.

It was situations like this that confirmed to him that he wasn't the one to deal with people. Give him a number every day, and they never get offended.

Fourteen

Conner had received the cold shoulder enough to know when it was happening to him. Riley was making sure she stayed in her lane, as it was. If there was a way to leave a room or his presence, she found it. He was surprised she didn't just put up a sign that said plague.

Every so often, James or Rose would look at him as Riley passed. Everyone knew there was something wrong, but no one wanted to bring it up as they were all unsure of the source of the trouble. In truth, what made it all the harder was that Riley was the epitome of politeness. If he had looked up the word, her picture would be there with a smile that showed a few teeth but not too much, and none of the warmth would have reached her eyes.

Conner thought a day would help cool things down, and maybe she'd forget. He even went to check on the sleigh his family would go on for Valentine's Day. After making sure the sleigh was there and the horses were in good condition, he went back into the house to see if he could find Riley. He wanted to find a way to apologize. If he could only get in the same room with her, he could try to repair his callousness.

Maybe he'd wait her out in the kitchen. She had to eat, and Riley always came in to check on Merlin. Conner saw Merlin and called to him. The dog eagerly turned and came to him.

"Merlin, I'm going to need some help. It seems as though I have messed up royally. If this keeps up, I'll be kicking you out of the proverbial dog house." Conner reached in his pocket to give Merlin a chicken treat, his favorite. Conner had made some decisions. He and Riley would, at the very least, get to be in the same room. He gave Merlin another treat, and the dog sat and looked up at him faithfully. "Good, I'm glad we understand each other. I'll keep you on the treat list, buddy, if you just help me with your mistress. Now let's go to lunch and see if she'll show."

"Merlin?" Riley called out.

Conner looked at the dog, who looked at the entrance to the kitchen, and then swung his head back towards Conner. Conner patted his leg, and Merlin took a step towards him and took a seat.

"It's show time, buddy," Conner said as they walked into the kitchen.

"Rose, is it that special time of the day again where you make a masterpiece and call it a meal?" he said as he walked into the kitchen.

"You're just trying to find out what's for lunch," Rose said to him, shaking her head. When Conner walked in, he headed toward the empty seat at the table, and Merlin followed. Riley's smile had gone stiff, and the light laughter that he had heard as he walked in dried up.

"Merlin, don't be a bother," Riley called. The dog picked up his head, but Conner smoothly patted his leg that was faced away from Riley. She didn't notice, but Merlin turned towards him and then sat down at his feet.

"Maybe Merlin needs a moment. Why don't you take a minute before you go off?" Conner said. "Soon, the house will be filled with people, and being able to sit at the table or talk will be impossible."

He could tell that she didn't see that as such a bad thing. It was on the tip of Conner's tongue to say that it wasn't an order, just a request, but the way things were, he was sure if he clarified his intent, she would leave the room.

"The inn looks amazing. It seems larger now and airier," he said.

"It's the change in lighting and using lighter colors on the couches with dark accent pillows. There are some potpourri shells as well that give off a citrus smell."

Rose laughed. "It looks like we have more than one person who can take what they've been given and get a bigger return."

Conner looked at Riley, who was still looking composed but ready to go.

"Yes, it's true. You don't know what you have until you start to work with it," Conner said.

Riley's back straightened, and he thought she'd just get up and leave.

"How are the horses?" she asked.

Conner smiled. "The horses are great. They're ready for their debut rides. I know you haven't been on a ride before. Maybe we can go to the Swan festival tonight? There's always one ride there before the releases."

He could see her whole body stiffen up.

"I don't know, there is still work to be done," she hedged.

"All of the town members would be there. I could put in an appearance and see how things are. I wouldn't go without you. I think your insight is better with the town's people than mine."

He saw the flash of temper cross her face and the indecision she was facing. He knew she was trying to avoid time with him, but she'd do what she could for the town.

"Okay, we can go for a bit," she said through a tight smile.

"Great, I'll come to get you in about four hours. I know the festival starts around seven. I think that will give us enough time to see the sights and the people."

Riley nodded and then stood up. "Well, if I'm going to be ready, I need to finish my work."

With that, she left the room. "You two need to work this out, Conner," Rose said.

"I'm trying."

"Try? Now, that is an odd word coming from you."

"Riley doesn't give me a lot of leeway."

"Well, it is my experience that when women give men the cold shoulder, it's because they've done something that is hurtful and callous."

Conner hung his head and closed his eyes. "I did. Since then, I've been trying to make it up to her. For a moment, I thought she would say no to going to the festival tonight.

I was feeling so desperate I would have asked you and James to come along."

Rose wiped her hands on the counter and went to stand in front of him. Conner looked up and saw Rose standing with her arms crossed. "Hear me, Conner. I care for you more than I should, but I respect Riley. If you had asked us, I would have refused. You need to handle the issues you are having with Riley head-on. If you two can't find a way to talk to each other when things are not great, then having a relationship is going to be just about impossible."

Rose gave him a nod and then left the room. When Rose walked toward the exit, Merlin got up to follow her. Conner patted his leg with the treats. Merlin looked over his shoulder and then continued to follow Rose out of the door.

"Where does that leave me when I have treats, and even the dog won't stay with me? I've got to do something right tonight, for both of our sakes." Conner said to no one at all.

Maybe there was still time to get sick. Riley knew she wasn't going to call in sick. She had agreed to go to this festival with Conner, and she'd do her duty and then come home. Home. What a word to say. Turtle Dove Inn wasn't her home. No matter how much work she put into it, it was still just a job.

Riley was proud of the work she had done. Reservations

were booked out for the next three months after the new brochures had gone out to the neighboring travel agencies. It had been a spot before, but the personal touches gave the inn a more old-world, romantic feel. She had so many ideas for the inn, but she had to remember she wasn't going to be here. Marjorie had said they would look into a bed-and-breakfast for her in town, and Riley would be able to pour herself into that.

Conner's parents would be here soon. She hoped they liked what she had done. It was so nerve-wracking waiting to see if the family of the man you had feelings for liked what you had done. In the end, wasn't that the problem? Riley had feelings for Conner that were not reasonable.

In some ways, she was hurt by his words in the car, but in retrospect, she needed them. She needed him to remind her that she was just staff. She might be staff that had confidential information, but she was staff nonetheless. When she thought about the argument in the car, she couldn't believe she was giving him advice on his family. He was so right. She was not an authority on family at all.

"Stop stalling, Riley," she murmured to herself. "Get out there, and let's get this done and over." When she came out of her room, he was ready and waiting.

"I'll get my keys," Riley said. Driving the truck might distract her a bit from being in the vehicle with him.

"No, I've already warmed up the car, and it's out front," Conner said.

Riley nodded. It seemed like it was all going well. In fact, it was going fine. Then when she stepped out of the door and saw the car, the incident came back to her. It was like she was returning to the scene of the crime. She took one step, and her breath started coming in short gasps. Riley stopped. She couldn't do this. It was time for her to rethink all of the excuses she said she wouldn't use before. Cramps, migraines, or maybe even her whole body was wracked in pain emanating from her heart. She had avoided cars all together while she had been here and now, after she thought she had given herself enough time, this was happening.

Then she heard a bark. She turned to see Merlin at the side of the house. He didn't come over; he was just standing there. It was all the clarity she needed. She and Merlin had been through worse. Was she really about to bail and let others down because her feelings would be in the way for a thirty-minute drive to a festival?

If worse came to worse, she could just look out the window like Merlin did. She knew the problem. Against all common sense, she had fallen for Conner Sanders. He was a recluse, a genius, and most times the most caring, considerate person she knew. Tonight she would hide her heart and try to just be in the moment. He would be gone soon, so she would at least have some decent memories of the two of them. They weren't the type of memories she wanted to start with in her new home town, but she'd play the cards she was dealt.

"Did you want me to drive?" she asked.

"I got it. Besides, what kind of impression would I be making to the town if I needed a woman to drive me to the festival?" Conner joked.

"I didn't realize your ego was so fragile," she replied.

"I would have thought by the way I've been acting; you would have known that I'm not as secure as I need to be."

Riley looked at Conner over the top of the car. "Is this about your security, Conner?"

He stopped and gave her a long look before answering. "It's about me trying to keep as much control as I can. It's not really doable, but I need to take a stab at it."

Riley gave him a sad smile. "I might understand that sentiment, but it shouldn't come at the expense of others."

"I'm sorry, Riley."

She looked at him and sighed. "Me too."

She got in the car and looked out the window, praying the tears wouldn't drop. She could breathe through them as long as he didn't speak right away.

As the car started, Merlin started barking. They both looked at him. Never had she been so happy for Merlin. Riley looked at Conner.

"Do you mind if we take him?"

He hesitated and then nodded yes.

Riley turned and opened the door for the back. "Merlin, let's go."

The dog loped over as if he had been waiting for the signal all along.

"Sorry," Riley murmured as they drove off.

"For?"

"Merlin."

She saw Conner smile. "Merlin is a new experience that I'm thrilled to have. I will admit I had some reservations, but Merlin has shown me how wrong I was."

Riley smiled. She didn't think Conner and Merlin would hit it off so well. Merlin didn't usually take to strangers.

They were at the fair in no time, and they got Merlin

out of the car. Fortunately, there was a spare leash in the trunk for him.

"Let's take a walk through the fair and see if we find anything for Merlin," Conner said.

Riley saw the crowd there and was amazed. "It never seems like there are this many people in town," Riley said in awe.

"They're here. Let's go and make ourselves known."

Riley stopped. "I don't know, Conner. There are a lot of people."

"Yes?"

"I didn't think it would be like this. They all expect you to save them?"

Conner gave a small smile. "These things rarely work out the way we think they are going to," he said.

"When Marjorie said what she did, it seemed like a much smaller job, but now—"

"Now, this is what it is. We're not going to run because the situation changes, are we Riley?"

"I'm not running. I'm just saying—"

Conner held out his hand. "Come on, Riley. Where is that spirit that practically accused me of sinking the whole town? I need your fight."

"Conner, can you really do anything for this town?"

"I think I can; otherwise, I wouldn't have come." He held out his hand, and she took it, Merlin going to his side as they walked.

A woman called out to Riley. She had tattoos on her arms, and it wasn't until she was closer to the woman that she recognized her from the cookie-rolling night.

"Hi, we've met but weren't formally introduced. I'm

Layla Granger. I'm glad the two of—I mean the three of you, made it. I was telling my brother, Ryan, that this festival is a double pleasure. The weather is holding, and we have a whole family of otters to release. Hard to have a releasing festival and have nothing to release.

"Hello Layla, I do remember you."

Layla laughed. "It's the tatts, right? No one has the same ones or so many."

Riley blushed. "They are beautiful. This is Conner Sanders, my uh—"

"Yes, the man who holds the whole world in his hands, if the rumors are to be believed."

Conner held out his hand. "I've heard you make pottery that sells very well here and online?"

"Did you?"

Riley looked at them both and decided they were at least civil, if not friendly.

"Were you scouting out the talent you could find in the bay, Mr. Sanders, to see if you could buy that as well?"

"No, Ms. Granger. It turns out my mother is a fan of pottery, and I wanted to find a place for her to visit while she was here."

Riley watched Layla's whole demeanor change when he said it was for his mother. "When your mother arrives, tell her to stop by. I'll have my kiln going and make something for her in mind.

"I'll make sure she gets to you. My dad will come to grumble about her not spending too much, but in the end, he'll give her whatever she likes."

Layla laughed.

"I've seen the syndrome with my own parents. It's

endearing and gives us all hope of what to aspire to. When you get a chance, you might want to get the funnel cake with strawberries on top. It usually sells out fast."

"Thanks for that heads up," Riley said.

"Ah, I see my brother giving the signal of help. I need to go rescue him from women who have discovered he's an artist and single," Layla laughed as she walked away.

There was an open picnic bench by the water bank, so they took a seat there, and Merlin seemed to be content with the place as well.

"Great spot, Conner, even Merlin likes it."

"I had to have some kind of win. I feel like I've been batting zero at a thousand miles an hour."

Riley reached out to his hand. "Hey, cheer up. Your family is coming, and they sound amazing. You are on the right track and doing the right thing.

Conner looked at their hands and then placed his over hers. He then looked up into Riley's eyes.

"I want to make it right all the way around. I know my business is numbers, but even more important, it means I can spot a good thing when I see it. And when I do, I do my best to hold to it. If it's possible. Is it, Riley?"

What was he doing? It was like Conner had not gotten the script of their relationship. Hold on? They didn't have a relationship. She had just fallen down the slippery slide of being in love with him. He was supposed to be the one with the sense and keep the distance between us. Then all of those rules went out of the window when he moved next to her and placed his arm around her. The weight of his arm seeped into her body and gave her a languid feel to the whole event.

"It seems like you've made the rounds, and people like you."

"I think I've just been in one or two of the right places with a couple of people who get around. I think you'd find that the people here at the bay are pretty friendly."

"I would disagree. When they look at you, they see the Mother Theresa, but when they look at me, they hide their children to make sure they're safe."

Riley thought Conner was exaggerating, but when she looked around the festival grounds, she caught one or two of the residents giving Conner a once over that could have almost been deadly. She was going to try to find something encouraging to say when they saw a bunch of lights going toward the bay. They could see the view from the bench. Conner pulled her closer and then pointed at the umbrella where cages were being brought out.

To think, when he had pulled her closer, Riley wondered how this kiss would go. So when he started pointing to the bank instead, she mentally shook herself and tried to focus on his words and not on the drugged feeling of being safe in Conner's arms.

"They are releasing a family of otters. I understand they've had the animals for about a month. It doesn't seem that long, but the group doesn't want to keep them too long so that they get used to a human's touch," Conner said.

Riley could definitely understand the dilemma of getting used to human touch. She was having the same problem. This type of weakness Riley had a problem with. She was fighting herself as well as the situation. She refocused on the bank and saw the telltale sign of water rippling and the glossy reflection of the otters as they turned on their backs and waited for their family members to catch up before they swam on.

"They're free," Conner said with a smile. "You want to go and find that funnel cake?"

Riley nodded. To be honest, she might have nodded to anything to get out of Conner's arms. She was convinced she couldn't fight the spell while she was in his arms.

"I'd love some food."

Fifteen

So now Conner knew what it would look like if he did a corporate takeover in a picnic area. Everywhere he went, he could feel the hostile gazes at his back. At one point, he thought about cutting the trip short because of the people, but Riley had said they were concerned, not aggressive, and right now, she was the expert when it came to the feelings of the people.

Inheritance Bay had two pros for Conner. The first pro was that it was the place where his parents had met, and so it had emotional significance. The other pro was that the bay had been identified by one of his departments as a potential place to build up an office that was low cost. He hadn't really thought about the second benefit, but now that he was here and had decided to help the town, he could see it was time to call Nolan to come to town for an evaluation.

He needed to meet with Marjorie and make some concrete arrangements so that everyone would know that he was serious. Conner had to admit that he made a lot of decisions by himself in front of his computers. When Riley had pointed out this issue, it also brought up the issue of him working in a group. This wasn't just a group or a department, these were families. He needed to think of them like his if he was going to do right by them.

Again, Riley was the one who had pointed this out to him. It was her awareness and compassion that he needed to temper his focus and drive. He had only been looking out for his family, but there had been other ways to do what he had done without being this extreme. Conner was going to do the right thing and help the bay get back to what it was.

He wasn't really looking at where they were going, so when Riley spoke, he jumped a bit.

"Funnels, and the line is short," Riley said, bringing him back to the present.

"Okay, let's get three. Two for us, and then one for Merlin," he said. Riley laughed at Merlin, who was looking up as if he knew what he was about to get.

"I see that Merlin has approved that message as well," Riley said.

Conner looked at the funnel woman who was smiling at them. Before he could order, she got in a question first.

"So how was our releasing? I know it wasn't like they do it in big cities, at least not the way I see it on the television."

"I thought it was so much better than the city releases. When they do it in the city you can't see the actual animals. Someone has to record it and then play it for the public to see. On top of that, they definitely wouldn't allow Merlin to attend."

"How many would you like?"

Conner held up three fingers, and the woman smiled as she reached behind her to bring two funnels out and then placed them in another in the fryer. Before Conner could ask for toppings, he heard a man behind him.

"So the big man gets to take everything in town? Working men need to get food so we can earn a living for as long as we can."

Conner knew the voice, but it was the words that put him on alert. He made sure to keep in shape in case he had to handle an altercation on his own. He never forgot the lessons of being in foster homes and orphanages. He didn't feel like it was going there, but he wanted to make sure Riley and Merlin were okay, so he wouldn't let his guard down.

"Larry, I didn't know you were closing the hotel. What did you want, Larry?" the woman asked.

"Well, Tina, I was hoping that you'd be able to serve a working person," Larry said.

"I'll get a fresh one right up for you," Tina said.

"Why don't you give me one of those you have on the shelf so I can go on my way," Larry asked loudly.

"Larry, the other ones are just about done. The new ones will be piping hot, so it'll be fresh by the time you get to the hotel."

"I can nuke it. I'll take those. Mr. Owns-the-Whole-Town can wait for the people who really work to get theirs first."

Conner knew where this was going, and after listening to Riley, he should have been grateful that this hadn't happened earlier.

"You're right, Larry. You do have to go back to work so you can have the funnel and go," Conner said.

"You telling me what to do now, rich man?" Larry said with a sneer in his voice.

Conner turned toward Larry and looked at Riley and Merlin standing to the side. He adjusted his plan of action and looked at Larry.

"I think you should take the cake and go. Otherwise, you may find that I no longer own just one-third of the town. I may add to my collection a hotel."

Larry looked at Tina and at Riley. He turned back to Conner, and he nodded.

"Thank you for understanding. I'm alone at the hotel, is all," Larry said as he reached for the cake. Then he reached in his pocket, and Conner stopped him.

"I'll pay for it, Larry. I don't want anything to hold you up."

Larry took the funnel and left. Tina looked at Larry's retreating back and shook her head. "I'm sorry about that, Mr. Sanders."

"Really, it's nothing. It's recently been brought to my attention how things are in town. I can't blame a person for wanting to vent a little."

Tina pulled out two funnels and topped them. When Conner got ready to pay for them, she smiled and said it was on the house. They were going back to the bench when Riley began.

"I can't believe he did that. You know Merlin didn't like him before, and Merlin is rarely wrong. I just can't believe he did that," Riley said as they took their seats. "I'm not sure what Marjorie is going to do but—"

"She's not going to do anything, Riley, because neither one of us is going to tell her," he answered.

"Is that another order from my boss?" she asked.

Conner shook his head. There were some days he just didn't think he could win. "It's not an order, and I was wrong to say it that way."

"What would have been a better way to make me stay quiet?"

Conner looked at Riley's profile. She was tense and rightfully upset. "Riley, please help me out. I should have asked your opinion."

She turned towards him. "Yes, you should have. I would have still said tell Marjorie."

"I've got to convince a town that I'm going to help them. I don't think telling on Larry is the way to go to start out the negotiations. No one was hurt, and we are here to help the situation. Let's let Larry be and focus on the town and not one man's anger."

She took a bite out of her funnel cake and then turned back to Conner.

"You're right, if you had said that, I would have agreed."

"Truce, Riley. This night is me trying to do this right," Conner said.

She nodded her head, and the both of them went back to eating the funnel cake. After a few moments, Layla came over and told them to see the arts and crafts.

"Maybe you'll see something for your mother, Mr. Sanders."

"Well, how can I turn that down?" Conner said.

Conner took Riley to the two-lane village façade.

Riley stopped at every stall and listened to the crafts-people. Her patience and compassion for each person was obvious and genuine. At first, when they saw Conner behind her, they were a bit nervous, but as Riley asked questions, he learned more and more about the town. They were artists and craftsmen who needed more exposure but didn't lack for talent.

Soon the evening air was getting chilly, and it was time to go home. Conner hated for the evening to end, but Riley's health had to come first. When they got in the car and were driving away, Riley spoke.

"Thank you, Conner. Tonight was amazing."

He smiled. He was glad he hadn't messed this up. He wished she had made the comment before he started driving, but he would take his wins were he could, Riley was the one. If he wasn't sure before, he was now. He could see forever with her and Merlin.

"I'm glad you enjoyed yourself. I worry that you work all the time and don't have any fun," he said.

"Decorating and preparing the inn is a lot of fun for me, Conner."

"Okay, let me say it a different way. I hope you get to do other things, not work-related, that are fun."

Riley laughed. "That is so funny coming from the man whose job is his fun."

"You've got me, but I realize everyone doesn't have that, and I want to make sure you are happy, Riley."

Conner hated the idea he was driving. He couldn't look at Riley and get an idea of how she was taking his words. Could she feel what he was feeling? Did she know where he was going with this?

"Conner, you are a special man. I have to tell you that being at Turtle Dove Inn has been one of the most unforgettable experiences in my life," she said. Fortunately, he had just driven up to the inn, so he was finally able to look at her.

"Wow, that sounded ominous," he said. Before Riley could respond, they were both startled when they heard Merlin snoring. They were both jolted. Riley looked in the back.

"I'm sorry. He's older, we can guide him in, but we need to be careful because sometimes he's grouchy."

Conner looked at Merlin and then Riley. He guessed this would have been a bad time to ask her for clarification before they took Merlin in. Instead, he smiled and offered to get him to her room.

Fifteen minutes later, they were both in her room, and Merlin was in his doggy bed.

Riley smiled and folded her hands across her chest. "Thank you for tonight. As you can hear, we both had a wonderful time," she said with a laugh.

This wasn't the way he wanted this to end. He needed more time, for what he wasn't sure, but he knew he needed more time.

"So why don't we end the night with a hot chocolate and marshmallows. I've got a secret stash of them, and the hot chocolate is Rose's recipe."

"You have a stash of marshmallows?"

Conner shook his head in mock despair. "You would not believe me if I told you how aggressive James can be towards the marshmallows. Will you have hot cocoa with me? I'm not ready for the night to end, Riley, are you?"

Sixteen

That was a loaded question if she ever heard one. What was she ready for? Riley knew how this was going to end. Common sense and self-preservation of her already compromised heart said that she should leave now.

Unfortunately, all the logic in the world wouldn't get her to end this dream night with him. She was going to have to carry this dream with her after he was gone and after this was over. Knowing she was too far gone not to be hurt, the woman in her wanted to dream a little longer.

This wasn't a relationship; it was a magical moment that no one would be able to explain. It would be the culmination of happenstance that gave them a chance to just be. Conner could just be an ordinary man who was attracted to a woman, and Riley could be a free woman not trying to start over attracted to a man who was kind, considerate, and intrigued her on an emotional, physical, and mental level.

All of those things put together meant there could only be one answer. "I'm not quite ready either, and I'll take you up on the chocolate. Although I'll warn you, I am considered a renowned chef when it comes to the art of making hot chocolate."

Conner laughed. "You had me worried there with the pause. I thought you were trying to find a way to say no to me, and here you were just wondering if you would be subjected to inferior chocolate."

Oh if you are going to live the dream then live it big.

"Lead the way, padawan. I'll look over your shoulder to see if you make any really rookie mistakes," she teased.

He held out his hand to her. "Come along, my pretty, I'll show you some of the best hot cocoa ever. It will spoil you for everything else and seal my place as the hot cocoa master."

Riley took his hand with a bittersweet smile. He was saying a statement that was truer than he knew.

"Well, then off we shall go," she said, taking his hand. The walk to the kitchen was short, and when they arrived, he showed her to a seat.

"Prepare to be amazed."

She watched him pull out containers and then empty one into a pot. "What are you doing? Cocoa is made from scratch."

"Ah, it is unless you know Rose made a batch for the morning crowd because some of the family will be here," Conner said.

"So you're not making it from scratch, you're cheating!"

Conner laughed. "I'm not cheating as I didn't commit to the process, just the end result. Ha!"

Riley laughed and went to stand by the stove. "It smells

divine. I'll make sure to give Rose my compliments," she said. It was everything she thought this would be. She and Conner joking as if there was only them. Her standing close to him. Close enough to smell the distinctive smell of Conner and funnel cakes. Determined to fight temptation, she went back to her seat.

Conner brought out cups and a bag of miniature marshmallows and put them on the table between them. Then Conner sat down at the table with her.

"Let the tasting begin," Conner said.

They took their first sips and then put the cups down. Riley looked up and saw the kid in Conner. She saw the devilish spark of the boy genius. She saw the man she loved. This last hurrah had been a mistake beyond imagining. She wasn't just indulging her heart for the last time; she was ripping it out. She had to get through this cup and leave.

"The chocolate is amazing. You have to tell Rose that I said so. I won't even try to make any now that I've tasted this."

Riley took another sip and looked over the rim of her cup, and drank him in. If Riley looked at their current situation, there would be no reason why this moment felt like the most romantic moment ever. It wasn't the cozy close quarters it was before. It was just two adults grinning over cocoa in an empty kitchen like children. No sly glances, no random but deliberate touches—it was just them.

"I'm surprised Rose hasn't shown up. She's usually psychic when I'm in the kitchen," she wondered out loud.

"Today before we left, Rose and James left to go check on her daughter. I believe her daughter is in the last part of her pregnancy and was having some difficulty. It's been on and off for a couple of weeks. I told Rose she could go whenever she wanted. Today the call came, and after her fretting, James came to me, and I sent them on the first flight out."

Riley put her mug down and looked at Conner, trying to find the words. Of course, he sent them. Family would always be first with him.

"Is there anything I can do?" Riley asked.

"No, it's all taken care of. The food is catered, and it'll be brought in, so the only thing that will need to be done is for it to be warmed up."

"They will be descending tomorrow then?"

"Yes, like a friendly locust horde," Conner said with a laugh. Riley looked into her cup, but there was only a scale of cocoa.

"Riley, I want you to know that although I seem to be the harbinger of bad to all things in Inheritance Bay, I've never been happier than the time you've been here.

"You aren't the harbinger. My, that is an S.A.T. word if ever I heard one. I'm happy that I came here too," she murmured.

His hand reached out across the table, open and waiting for hers. Riley looked from his hand to his eyes. She'd already passed commonsense, and this was just icing on the cake. She placed her hand in his. He put his cup aside, and they both stood up.

"I think I should be going to bed now," she murmured without moving away from him.

"I think our kiss has been on my mind so much so, I've renamed it The Incident," he joked.

Riley looked up at him and could feel the gentle sway of her body towards his. There was throwing caution to the wind, and then there was throwing caution into the flame.

"It's been on my mind too."

"Shall we test if it was just a moment?" he asked.

Here he was giving her control, and she was gathering memories for when there was no more *them,* and he was gone. She reached out and pulled him into the kiss. She embraced a future she could never have and a man she would love for a very long time. He tasted of cocoa and marshmallows. She'd never look at marshmallows the same again.

The first kiss had been a surprise, a hidden moment that was just the right time. This kiss was deliberate, deep, and moving. There was a slow perusal about this kiss as she remembered every contour of his lips and the feel of his shoulders. Riley was painting a mental canvas of this event, and she spared none of her senses to do it. The longer they kissed, the deeper the ache became. She had to hold it back until she broke the kiss between them.

"So that's what happens when you plan on kissing Conner Sanders," she said with a smile. "I won't have that question running around in my head, now will I?"

He lifted her chin and looked into her eyes, and she almost cried. He looked like a mischievous boy with a secret.

"But have we really explored what happens when you kiss me? Maybe we need more practice runs?" he asked.

"I really have. The first kiss was enough to send you running. A girl has to know if a guy is running for the hills because it was the worst, or is he running away because the kiss was so good it made him lose control."

Conner laughed and then placed his hand dramatically over his heart.

"I can solemnly swear that I ran because I was confused. I didn't want to take advantage of your situation, but I was completely enthralled."

"Enthralled? Wow, you've been boning up on your vocabulary. A man has never told me that, so you get first prize. Regardless, it was the best first and last time ever."

"The best, I agree," Conner said.

"Yes, well…"

Then Conner pulled her into his embrace. His hands ran up and down her spine, and the warmth of his breath fanned her ear. Each pass he made on her back made her relax more and more into him. It wasn't until she felt the slow nibbling on the shell of her ear that she brought her hands up.

"Conner, please," she whispered.

He stepped away, his chest rising and falling with the effort it took him to take a step back.

"Riley?"

She could see he was so confused. This was going to be one of the hardest things she ever did.

"You are an amazing person, Conner. You're more than I thought you would be. I like kissing you, and Merlin likes you. However, I realized that when my dad died, I didn't want to be with someone who wouldn't be with me completely. I need someone who cares enough to share with me."

"You don't think I'm that person?"

Riley let out a breath and then took a step back. "Conner, you are a self-made man. You solve problems all day long. You act first and then bring everyone else up to speed on what is going to happen. And you know what? I wouldn't change a thing about that. I wouldn't change a thing about you. The thing is, I wouldn't change a thing about me either."

"Well, you don't leave a lot of options for me. You seemed to have figured out who I am and what I can and won't do."

Riley reached out and ran her finger down his jaws. "Conner, be real here. You are the head of a company called Wealth Builders, so you make decisions about people's lives every day. You shoulder that responsibility, and you take care of others. It doesn't allow for you to have a committee."

"I have a board, Riley. I can talk to others. You're not giving us a chance. What you've done at Turtle Dove is amazing. My parents will be amazed, and I'm sure it will be an anniversary they won't forget."

Riley listened to him ramble and go all around the issue. "So what about talking to your family about your ex?"

"I'm handling it, Riley."

"But if I said yes to this relationship, it would be about us, right?"

"Of course."

"Your family would be my family, right?"

"Yes, they will absolutely adore you!"

"So we make decisions about our family, together?"

Conner ran his hands through his hair and walked away until he was in the middle of the kitchen.

"This thing with my ex is…"

"Is what Conner? A one-off? If it's not this, it would be something else. No matter what it is, it still leaves me on the outside. So I think the best thing we can do is get through your parents' visit, and then we can go our separate ways."

"That's it? Not even friends, Riley?"

Riley looked at him and gave a big sigh. "Friends Conner? Can we really just be friends?"

"I'm asking, Riley. Isn't that a step in the right direction? Please don't just leave me high and dry here."

Riley smiled and shook her head. "I should say no."

"Please."

"Fine, friends. It's probably a bad idea, but I can't imagine ending such a perfect night on a bad note."

"I might disagree with you on the note, but I'm happy with friends."

"Okay, that's all I've got, Conner. I'll see you tomorrow."

Riley didn't wait for Conner to say goodnight. She had to make it to her room before the heat behind her eyes spilled down her cheeks. She'd speak to Marjorie after the Sanders left. She was good to her word. She'd stay until the evening was over, and then after that, for her sake, she'd have to move on. Riley got dressed in her night-clothes and then lay in bed and pulled up the sheets. This might be the last time she did this. Depending on how the day ended, she might be able to leave tomorrow evening. She'd play it by ear because Conner might be able to be friends, but her heart was already too far gone for friends.

Seventeen

Conner had called Nolan. He would get him on the job of assessing Inheritance Bay. Between this and something else he had been working on, all of his spare time had been eaten up. His latest project was a challenge to his nature and a bridge to his future. He knew he'd have to split his attention soon. His family would be here.

When he closed the file, he realized the morning had totally slipped by while he had been in his office working. He wanted to make sure that all was ready and that Riley didn't need anything. He knew his family could be loud and a bit overbearing, but they were exactly what he needed when he was growing up. He couldn't wait for them to meet Riley.

As he walked to the kitchen, he realized it was closer to the afternoon. There was no need to worry. Riley had taken care of everything. She had gone over the checklists. The truth of the matter was he couldn't remember a time when he was so excited to see someone who wasn't family. Riley gave him a boost for the day and put him in a frame of mind that said it would all be okay.

After last night he had been giving some considerable thought to what she had said. He'd also been thinking that Riley was so much a part of his day to day he couldn't really imagine not finding her for lunch or not going for a walk with her and Merlin. He stood in the doorway, watching her in the kitchen. She was making a sandwich. Even the most basic things she did called to him, and he wanted to join.

She picked up her head and saw him there, and a warm smile greeted him.

"Hey, did you want a sandwich?"

"No, I'm on my way to get the clan. I wanted to tell you the inn looks amazing."

"Now? You're going now? I thought I had more time," she said as she wrapped up her sandwich.

"Don't worry, it will take us about an hour to get them all and bring them here. We're taking two cars."

"Good, the caterers and wait staff are on their way, and it will be set up for you when you get back," Riley said as she counted off items on her fingers.

Conner smiled. "So you're going to be ready for the Valentine's ride?" he asked.

"Ready?"

"Yes, you know it'll be about forty minutes. We'll be riding around the inn and then come back for some marshmallows and hot cocoa if I know my family."

"Well, I'll be in my room reading, so there is no getting ready for me."

"Really, Riley, don't make me go alone. Everyone will have someone. Can you just sit with me so they don't harass me?"

"You've got to be kidding! Listen, Conner we talked this over, and it's best if we keep it professional and—"

"Fine, come so you can hear what they think about the inn."

Riley stopped and gave him a stern glare. "We're reaching a bit here, aren't we?"

"I'm just saying you're not going to know if you just skip out on me tonight," he said as he moved to stand next to her.

Riley sighed and gave him a side look. "This is the problem. You can't get your way all the time."

"If I did, this conversation would be going in a totally different direction."

Riley threw up her hands. "Fine, you win."

Conner turned her chin towards him. "I haven't won, but I'm working on it." With that, he placed a quick kiss on her lips and then pulled back to smile at her. "I've got to go now, but try not to run away from me before I get back."

"I'm not running. I'm saving us."

Conner reached over and picked up half of her sandwich. "Don't bother trying to save me. I'm happy being a goner for you."

"Young lady, where do you think you're going?" asked Steven Sanders. Riley thought his voice sounded like some Olympic God, deep and smooth. It was loud enough for everyone to hear, but he wasn't yelling. It could almost be comforting if it weren't for the fact she was trying to get away.

"Oh, don't mind me. I thought I'd catch up on a book while you all—"

"Nonsense, we all need to go on a ride after all that food. It'll help the digestion," Steven said.

"The ride is for you all to spend some time—"

"Now, now, young lady, you can stop trying to convince me otherwise. The more, the merrier, and I can see your touch everywhere here. I wanted to thank you for it. I've been with Portia more than thirty years, but coming back to the Turtle Dove looking lived in and active, made it feel like we met just yesterday."

Riley nodded and then left the kitchen before she embarrassed herself. Oh, she could see where Conner got his sense of style and persuasion from. As she was walking out, a statuesque woman stopped her.

"Hello Riley, I know it's hard to get all of our names right, but I'm Grace. Or, the only one with blonde hair," the woman said with a laugh. Riley remembered her as the one who watched over everyone when they came into the inn and offered to help with anything. Riley liked her.

"Hello Grace, how can I help you?"

"Everything is great. I was just wondering if you could help a nosy older sister out."

"Okay, I can try. Go for it."

"Is Conner having a life crisis? He's young, but I hear it can happen to successful men as well."

"I'm sorry," Riley said, hoping she had on an appropriate look of confusion.

"Conner invited us all here. I mean, he always goes all out for our parents' anniversary, but we usually just hear about it. This year we all get an invite. What gives?"

Riley nodded and then extended her hands to encompass the inn. "I know he put a lot of effort and work into getting the inn up to speed."

"I agree," Grace said. "However, that still doesn't answer the question why here and now? My brother doesn't do surprises, so there is some logical answer that more than likely has to do with money or numbers."

A voice came from behind Riley, and she had to keep herself together in order to not jump when she heard the soothing tone come unexpectantly from behind her.

"And just where is my boy?" Portia Sanders asked.

Riley wanted to ask the same thing, but she knew the answer. Again this was just another reason that reassured her that they couldn't be together. Here was his family, and he was indulging in his project.

"I'm sure he'll be out soon. He had some last-minute project details to address," Riley said.

Grace put her arm around Portia. They walked towards the coat room to get ready for the ride.

"Come on, Mom, you know how Conner is, we will all find out when he's good and ready."

As they went to get their coats, Riley turned to quickly find Conner, but she didn't have far to go. She walked right into his chest, only to have his arms close around her.

"Umph!" Riley said as Conner stabilized her.

"You could have just told me you wanted to be back in my arms," Conner joked. Riley didn't answer at once because a part of her was rejoicing at being in his arms again.

"I was not," Riley said in mock outrage. "I was looking for you because your family is wondering why you gathered them and then left them for work. And so you know your mom and big sis wanted to know what I know about you acting out of character."

"Hmm, and I suppose you told them they'd have to take it from your cold dead hands," he said, imitating a pirate.

She shoved him aside. "No, silly. I did not, but this trip—while both of your parents seem to adore it—has definitely made them ask a question or two about your behavior."

Conner sighed. "Now you know."

"Know what?"

Conner grabbed her by the waist and spun her around. "Now you know why it's so important for you to come with us on the ride. You can't leave me to them. They scare me," he said with big puppy dog eyes.

Riley grinned at him. "Really, you expect me to fall for such a blatant ploy?"

Then they both jumped when Steve Sanders came from behind them.

"That's right, gal, don't fall for that silliness. Make him work for it," Steve Sanders said.

"Dad, whose side are you on?"

"I'm on the woman's side, boy, that's always the

winning side. You're just not old enough to know that yet." Steve said, laughing as he walked off.

Riley turned toward him and placed her hand over his mouth. "Gather your troops. Let me get Merlin, and I'll be right out. Not a word from you."

"I live to obey," Conner said.

"I wish," Riley murmured.

Eighteen

He was almost done with this project, but once again, the time had passed him by. After the ride last night, Riley had tried to sneak off. The family finally convinced her to stay one more day with them with the bribe of telling all the embarrassing stories they could find about him.

Conner thought it was a small price to pay. He was almost ready. He had come out of his office thinking that everyone would be in the kitchen with the cocoa. Instead, he just found his dad sipping on cocoa.

"So, the bear has come out of the cave. Is he searching for food or a person is the question?" The sound of his dad's voice was a welcome find.

"I've already found gold, Dad. Where did they all go? Conner asked.

"I'd say your little lady has pegged them all accordingly and has dropped them in different parts of the house doing different things. Your brother is watching some war movies in a theatre room, your mother and Grace are plotting next Christmas already, and the rest of your sisters are catching up. I'd say everyone is properly occupied."

"Riley is good at that, reading people and helping them get what they want." Conner didn't know it until that moment, but it was necessary for his dad to like Riley. It wouldn't have stopped anything he had planned, but with it, he felt like he was invincible.

She was a joy to everyone. He knew she believed they had some steep climbs to overcome, but he had a plan, and if it all went well, they'd all be happy.

"So what are you making in your office, new money?"

Conner had the grace to look sheepish. "I'm working on a special project."

"They are all special projects," Steve laughed. "I know you, but I would remind you that you need to attend to those around you if you want them to stay."

Conner thought about his dad's words. He didn't want to stay, and he didn't want to be alone. It was easier and safer to be single and working on his finance software. He could see that safety had a price. He didn't want to live out his days alone. Conner didn't want to miss out on one more day of Riley.

"Son, in case I didn't say it. Thank you for this. Your mother and I have walked the halls to bring back memories, and they came back as if they had happened yesterday. It seems your little woman knows what she is about."

"She does."

"She's got a great dog, you know," Steve Sanders said with a laugh. "Are you smart enough to grab an opportunity like that right in front of you?"

"I'm working on it," Conner said with a chuckle. "And

let me answer for Mom so she doesn't have to make a separate trip and hunt me down. I do care about Riley." Actually, Conner knew that he loved Riley, but he thought it would be remiss of him to tell someone else before he told her. He knew everything had to be just right to win Riley over.

"It's good to know all that genius thinking didn't eat up the commonsense," Steve laughed.

"Well, it didn't eat mine, but the problem is she doesn't want me. She thinks I have some personality flaws."

On that note, Steve laughed out loud and then took a drink of his cocoa.

"Well, then this is the woman for you. Did you tell her you're a genius and you love to figure out puzzles?"

Conner smirked. "I didn't say it, but I don't think it would have mattered."

"Well, whatever you're going to do, you'd best do it soon. Your mother and I would like to leave here knowing that calming heads have prevailed."

Steve got up and left the room with Conner sitting in the chair. No pressure, just his family looking at him to make sure he could get Riley. He had a call with the lawyers in ten minutes. Regardless of how that went, he had a game plan, and the end goal was Riley.

Later Conner managed to find Riley.

"Conner, I can say goodbye to everyone in the morning. This meal should be a family affair," she argued.

"Really, you need to be there. Besides me, everyone wants you to be there. They are so grateful for everything you've done that it would be odd if you weren't there for the final dinner."

Riley was nodding yes, but her heart was breaking. Being at the dinner would be all the family and experiences she would never have. It was another nail in the coffin, but it was for Conner, and so she found herself saying she'd be there.

"Conner, you are going to show, right? You've been holed up in your room forever. It seems that if you put this all together, you'd want to enjoy it with them."

"I hear a bit of censure in that voice, and I can't say a thing because you're right. Yes, I'll be there."

His words went through her as she went to his office. He was probably lost in his work. She went to the door and knocked on it. When she entered without him knowing, she heard him say, "I think those are at least the beginning numbers we can do. Thank you all so much for staying on the call." Then he hung up the phone, and she cleared her throat.

He spun around, and for a moment, he looked a bit lost.

"Conner, it's time," she murmured. Conner stood up, and the blue screen on the computer accentuated the dark spots under his eyes. "You look like crap."

"I know you won't believe it now, but your no-holds-barred speech is attractive to me."

"Trying to control everything is bad for your health."

"Your right, and I'm working on it. Care to go to dinner?"

"Changing the subject," Riley said.

"No, just employing a stalling tactic until I can regroup with my horde who will provide cover," he said with a smile.

"Fine, let's go."

Usually, Conner loved the reveal day of a new product. He loved the unveiling and the reactions from the crowd regardless of what it was. He tried to look at this family dinner the same way. His mom and dad were here. His siblings were here, and most importantly, Riley was here with Merlin waiting expectantly under the table. When everyone was accounted for, he nodded to his dad.

When Steven Sanders stood up, everyone else quieted down.

"I wanted to speak before we dig in. First, let me say thank you to Conner, who outdid himself with the Turtle Dove Inn. Your mother and I had good times here—"

Then his older brother Andrew interrupted. "Dad, remember we were all delivered to the door, so we are all of the firm belief that mom is as pure as the driven snow and you two have a fulfilling platonic relationship, don't take that from us," he moaned.

Everyone at the table laughed.

"Don't be too smart, kid, or I'll tell you which bedroom was your mother's and mine when we came here."

"Oh, no!" Andrew looked to Conner. "Please tell me none of the original beds are here," he playfully moaned.

Conner smirked. "The only one who knows the answer to that is Riley."

Steve held up his hand.

"Before Drew gets away with himself. Speaking of Riley, we want to thank you as well. Conner only has money, no sense of style or comfort. If it were up to him, we would all get electronics and text one another at the table. So we thank you for bringing love and life to the inn.

"As is the tradition on our anniversary, in each one of your seats, there was an envelope with your name on it. It's our gift to you. We know it's our anniversary, but you were our dream and hope from the beginning. You are the living example that it's not blood that holds a family together but love, trust, and loyalty. Eat well knowing you are in the company of loved ones."

As soon as Steve sat down, Conner stood up. "Before you all descend on the food. I need to say something."

"I knew there was something," Portia murmured loud enough for the table to hear, and for a moment, Conner almost thought about sitting down. Then he found Riley, and she gave him a nod.

"I gathered everyone here for the anniversary for two reasons. One of them was I wanted to give Mom and Dad an experience they would never forget because they have given so much to us all.

"I had also hoped to present a fiancée to this meeting, but that didn't work out. In fact, it worked out so poorly she is trying to blackmail me into paying her hush money. When I found out my relationship was over, I thought I could protect you all by having us together in a place no one could get to us.

"None of it is working out the way I thought. I'm glad Mom and Dad love the inn. I seem to have adopted a town, and my ex has decided to settle quietly."

First, there was shocked silence, and then they all started talking, and Conner answered every question thrown at him.

"Conner, a money-grubbing ex? You should have told us. We have all been there," Grace said.

"Don't pay," the older twin, Stella, said. "If you haven't sent the money, we can probably bargain her down more." Her twin, Willow, nodded in agreement.

Andrew shook his head. "Wow, baby brother, a woman. You should have told me. I could have wined and dined her for you."

Everyone laughed at the table. Then his mother cleared her throat, and there was silence.

"Conner, we're family. We don't need to be protected, but I know you did it out of love. Remember, when you love, it means being vulnerable and sharing no matter what light it puts you in. I'm a bit hurt you waited so long, but I'm so grateful you came to your senses and told us."

Steve put his hand over his wife's. "We're proud of you, Conner. We're proud of all of you. Now let's eat before the dog decides waiting for scraps is a losing game."

Conner watched all of them dig in, and he caught Riley's eye. She was smiling, and happiness shone in her eyes. Yes, he had made the right decision. Now he just had to close the deal.

Nineteen

This was going to be goodbye. Riley knew that Conner wanted to meet in his office after dinner, probably to come up with some new excuse as to why she should stay, but she had made up her mind. She was so proud of him for what he had done at dinner. Maybe if they had gotten it together before she had told him there was no chance of them being together, it would be different, but now she was just prolonging the agony. She didn't want to be here when his family left tomorrow. Riley thought she'd just leave tonight with Merlin.

Conner came into the room with a tray and two cups of cocoa. She looked at the cups, and memories of their closeness came back to her. Would she always have these thoughts when she was around hot cocoa? She'd probably have to stop drinking it for a little while until she could look back on this period without sadness.

"Thanks for coming, Riley. I know it's late, and I needed to talk to you." She looked at him, and again, she couldn't help but notice how he was still looking a bit tired.

"Conner, we can always do this some other time when—"

"No, I need to do it now. My father gave gifts to us all. I have a gift for you."

"No, Conner, I can't take it. I'm not a part of—"

"My parents gave us a present, and I have one for you. Just open it, Riley, please."

It was the size of a book, and she opened it. It was a bit thin, but maybe it was about dogs. She tore away the paper, and it was a set of what looked like diagrams and pictures.

"Computer notes?"

Conner made a face. "Those are the documents for the new application I built. It was your idea, so the app is yours. It's called Haggle. It evaluates a situation and then gives suggestions on how to haggle if it's feasible. You were right, asking others is a better way to leverage what everyone knows. I built the app, but this was all your idea."

Riley had her hand over her mouth. "Why, Conner?"

"I build stuff and solve problems. I don't haggle, and a lot of others don't either but we would if we knew how. This app will give you your independence, so you don't need to work for me or anyone. So you'll be free to choose."

Riley laughed and then went into his arms. "You are totally amazing, Conner. I love you."

"Are you sure?"

"Yes, I'm sure, and I don't need an app to help me out either."

Conner made sure that everything was out of the way

and held on to Riley. "I'm glad you're sure because I've been in love with you since that first kiss. However, this moment would have been very uncomfortable if you weren't in love with me."

"Conner, what are you talking about?"

He pulled back and gave her a white envelope. "What's this?"

"Our present from my parents. It seems that my dad was not as sure that my genius and creativity extended to letting you know how I feel."

Riley was still confused until she opened the envelope and saw a blank check. In the memo portion, it read *Make sure the ring is a good size.*"

Riley smiled. "I'm thinking something is missing," she said as she put the check back in the envelope.

She saw him hesitate. "You said you loved me, and you can't take it back."

Riley shook her head and then pulled his head to hers and placed a gentle kiss on his lips. "I'm yours, Conner, but you need to ask something," she said, trying to give him a hint.

Then it came to him, and his eyes widened. "Riley, would you do me the honor of being my wife?"

Riley nodded. "A little late on the asking. Out of order in the presentation, but I won't haggle with you on it."

"Thank goodness. I don't have a prototype, and I have a feeling I'd need it with you."

He laughed and kissed her, giving her hope, a new family, and a relationship where both of them would listen to and love one another.

I hope you enjoyed *Love at Turtle Dove Inn*. Check out *Love at Eagle Station*, book two in the Inheritance Bay Series.

If you'd like to get more news from me sign up to my newsletter to receive updates on new releases, sale promotions, and free books.

susanwarnerauthor.com

If you enjoyed this book, you could check out some of my other series:

Love Happens series. Sweet small-town romances that show that love could be waiting for you right around the corner.

Love Endures series. Clean and Wholesome love doesn't just happen in small towns, they can happen in cities too. Second chance love stories that prove that love endures.

Silver Fox series. Love comes to us in all stages of life. Celebrate the couples that find life after kids have grown up and sometimes even after our first loves have passed.

Love Saves series. Sweet romantic comedy where couples find out what really matters in their lives, how opposites can do more than just attract and how love can save us all.

Inheritance Bay Series. Inheritance Bay is a town that needs an influx of people to keep it from dying. A call is sent offering a second chance to former residences to come back home. The people who respond are coming to Inheritance Bay lured by the prospect of a second chance and the opportunity to leave their old lives behind. However the newcomer's to the bay will find redemption, safe harbor and in some cases an inner strength they didn't know they had. What's for sure is they'll get their inheritance of finding an uncondtional love that'll last a lifetime.

Hidden Treasures. (Coming Soon) Hidden treasures is a tourist town that specializes in romantic getaways. However, there is a club of women who call themselves the Liberated Damsels. They're women who have loved and lost. Now they are regaining their independence and confidence. Walk with them as they discover that taking a chance on love is worth it if the other person can see the hidden treasure within.

susanwarnerauthor.com

Made in the USA
Middletown, DE
26 October 2021

51037368R00102